'The Seed'
'Anu – Nexus'

Andrew David Doyle

Copyright © 2023 **A.D Doyle Publishing**

All rights reserved. No part of this publication may be reproduced, distributed, or transmitted in any form or by any means, including photocopying, recording, or other electronic or mechanical methods, without the prior written permission of the publisher, except in the case of brief quotations embodied in critical reviews and certain other noncommercial uses permitted by copyright law. For permission requests, write to the publisher, addressed "Attention: Book Rights and Permission," at the address below.

Published in the United States of America

ISBN 978-1-960684-28-8 (SC)
ISBN 978-1-960684-27-1 (Ebook)

A.D Doyle Publishing
222 West 6th Street
Suite 400, San Pedro, CA, 90731
andrewddoyle@hotmail.com

Order Information and Rights Permission:

Quantity sales. Special discounts might be available on quantity purchases by corporations, associations, and others.
For details, contact the publisher at the address above.

For Book Rights Adaptation and other Rights Permission. Call us at toll-free 1-888-945-8513 or send us an email at admin@stellarliterary.com.

Acknowledgements:

In bringing these stories together it often takes a more holistic approach to the characters and their fashionable lifestyle and elements of their psyche that are portrayed within the work. With that in mind I must, therefore, thank the undermentioned for their kind permission in allowing me to 'employ' and grab at their unique individual traits and embellish them with my points of view to achieve the make - up of the characters that I have in mind for this particular story, and for that liberty I thank them all respectively for their insights. This acknowledgement also extends to the technical world of search engines such as Google and Wikipedia which has provided a great resource to gain the valuable insights to the many places and ancient people that have shaped the modern world.

Characters:

An'Laara - Miss Loreta Alfafara, Filipina, living in Qatar

An Gregaar – Mr Greg Doliente, Filipino, living Qatar

Character Captain - Mr Mike Will, Scottish, Living in Qatar

Dedicated to:

William Alexander Buchan, Dundee, Scotland, born 12/08/1960 Died: 1st December 2022. Sometimes it is difficult forget who your real family are.

Contents

Chapter One: 'The Beginning' 1
Chapter Two: 'An Mer' 5
Chapter Three: 'Nibiru' 10
Chapter Four: 'Lilith the Scientist' 12
Chapter Five: 'Overthrow' 14
Chapter Six: 'The Seed – An'Mer' 16
Chapter Seven: 'Mars' 19
Chapter Eight: 'Mum's the Word' 21
Chapter Nine: 'Boxed Criminals' 25
Chapter Ten: 'Breakout' 30
Chapter Eleven: 'Darpa' 35
Chapter Twelve: 'Antartica' 39
Chapter Thirteen: 'God's Deadly Garden' 41
Chapter Fourteen: 'Arrival' 44
Chapter Fifteen: 'An Gregaar' 47
Chapter Sixteen: 'The Covenant of the Anunnaki' 50
Chapter Seventeen: 'Antigen' 57
Chapter Eighteen: 'Stichin's Flying Machines' 59
Chapter Nineteen: 'Dendera' 62
Chapter Twenty: 'An Freya' The Valkyrie Woman' 74
Chapter Twenty – One: 'Encounter' 80
Chapter Twenty – Two: 'The Hybrid An' Goose' 86
Chapter Twenty – Three: 'The theft of the Covenant Star
　　　　　　　　　　　　　Stones – Axum' 90
Chapter Twenty – Four: 'Bio Geometry' 93
Chapter Twenty – Five: 'Fly with me' 96

Chapter Twenty – Six: 'Intercept' 103
Chapter Twenty – Seven: 'Talking with God' 106
Chapter Twenty – Eight: 'Sushi Patrol' 109
Chapter Twenty – Nine: 'Warning' 116
Chapter Thirty: 'Assault' 118
Chapter Thirty – One: 'The Grand Illusion' 131
Chapter Thirty – Two: 'Setting the records Straight' 137

Preface

In ancient times long before the great biblical floods had struck across the third rock from the sun, the indigenous population of the planet Earth had finally woken up and had acknowledged that the Anunnaki space people who had arrived many centuries earlier from a distant planet known as Nibiru, were in fact now a very powerful and controlling '**alien**' society.

These space travellers had visited the planet in their flying chariots and magic carpets whilst planning to mine the vast quantity of valuable gemstones and mineral deposits that lay hidden in the underground caverns and chambers of most middle eastern countries across the planet earth. The strategy for this great journey across the stars was also a quest in order to acquire one important mineral called '**gold**' for their technical use, and then concentrated on the recovery of diamonds, salt and fresh water.

It was during this historical era that the lands of ancient Babylon, Akkadia, Mesopotamia, Egypt, Turkey and Sumeria amongst several other countries had been targeted as the start points for these star traveller excursions. Of course, whilst delivering their grand master plan in order to, not only mine for minerals but also to deliver the Anunnaki '**Human Agenda**. It was a plan involving multiple DNA experiments and manipulation designed to advance a human workforce from within the existing indigenous races of people.

The desired end result would be a population that would evolve with many great technological and life changing advancements created along with many scientific breakthroughs. These were planned staged events that had emerged systematically in the grand Anunnaki construct. And in time this life's new model had also created several great rifts and arguments across the incumbent ancient religious fractions leaders with their beliefs being either destroyed, moderated or simply eradicated amongst the many nations and their leaders who rebelled against their overlords, where subsequent horrific wars had erupted. And ultimately ended in mass bloodshed as false icons of worship fell into the sands of time but, especially more so as the Anunnaki mindset and promethean ideological attitude took an iron fist grip on the masses and had suddenly changed the many lives for the rapid expansion of the global population.

It was a construct that also affected the evolution of the Igigi people themselves, the Igigi also being a species who were an older hybridisation alien species program on the planet Nibiru. And, therefore, we should note that with any **'era'** or the passage of time there is always going to be a great amount of controversy or argument regarding ancient myths, conjecture, stories, fables and legends that were accompanied by great endeavours in human and Anunnaki history.

And we may also discover a multitude of great historical and colourful figures and characters emerging in these pre biblical and tumultuous times with many more unexplained revelations that will arise as future time unfolds. The details of which are going to be argued over by the modern scholars and historical boffins as they each lay claim to their own unique discoveries. Although in most cases certainly the majority of events are perhaps inexplicable, but, more so regarding the accounts as far as the Anunnaki are concerned of which were highly important.

But difficult to corroborate due to the lack of hard evidence or detail available regarding the species themselves as a range of colonies residing on our planet. And we should, therefore, understand that the **star people** in their tenure had also executed a multitude of horrific, violent and satanic acts coupled with their astral ritual ceremonies including human and animal sacrifice along with countless wars in their wake as a dominant invading species as they laid down their advanced strategies. We may also have to acknowledge that many strange anecdotes or ancient stories designed to capture the purest of hearts and minds of mortal man have been created in the **Anu**'s (Anunnaki) enduring legacy of existence whilst also attempting to stamp their amazing Anunnaki authority and history over mankind. And such events in those bygone days may well leave modern day scholars with a rather large and very complex itch to scratch, even more so as they each try and piece together the complex human jigsaw map of the human creation, whilst sifting through the complex library of ancient data accounts and information which have been passed up through the centuries, true or otherwise.

As we understand human folklore today in the twenty first century which is generally based on loose historical facts or perhaps fanciful notions or ideas about the human evolution theory is that we may find more often than not that fictitious accounts have certainly been very eloquently constructed. And subsequently, delivered to the masses by either word of mouth or in figurative sketches and art that is captured and recorded in many such wonderful ways as had the Sumerian cuneiform scripts. Intriguing accounts that were depicted by highlighting Egyptian hieroglyphs, monoliths and other great stone structures which are all excellent physical undeniable examples.

Each revelation based on its own merit being a record and testimony of many important events that may or may not have occurred. Thus, bringing into the limelight the many people entangled within this great web of mystery. Which in essence, consists of a vast library of detail available that should be digitally collated and structured in order to decide on a fixed definitive timeline for the real human evolution theory. Albeit, not forgetting that the great pyramid structures themselves are a wonderous testament to the storyline of ancient information, and their real number of pyramid styled buildings that are dotted across the globe which stems to about nine hundred if not more. Although, we should also know that within these buildings we shall also observe a **'kernel of real truth'** in these fantastic depictions. But scholars should also remain mindful as history is not always quite what it appears to be, and normally only recorded by the powerful or the victorious, or those more educated scholars.

The real caveat being that man must step back and look at the course of human history in far greater detail and not be side blinded or duped by modern day accounts of ancient history and perhaps take a deep scholarly look at the lies and misdirection first, where such accounts have been **drip fed** to humankind to describe or explain many events even before the so-called biblical times by several thousand years. And hitherto, we must consider the interventions or at least acknowledge that **aliens** per se as part of this process. Therefore, a sense of caution must also be applied and not just thrown into the wind when the subject matter concerns the enduring existence of the **Anunnaki** species, where the law of deception and misdirection may well run deep and hidden by the fabric of deception by human political powers of these modern times.

Author Narrative

This fictional narrative sets the pace for this highly controversial storyline around the amazing subject of the **Anunnaki** space people and their mysterious appearance on the planet earth several thousand years ago. In human history it was foretold that a great Princess known as Lilith had stopped over on the planet Mars during her space journey to earth from the planet Nibiru and had discovered to her great horror that anarchy had already occurred on the remote red planet and the newly deposed Anunnaki King Alalu was already dead. The monarch having being executed in the most of horrific and violent of ways imaginable to the human psyche having had his limbs literally torn apart by the power of the mythical Tiamat beast the 'She' The Serpent creature – or the serpent of the stars. Tiamat also being the name for a broken moon that could have been almost destroyed in astral antiquity and the planet's disintegration and could have formed into the planet we call home or mother earth. Although for most of Alalu's courtiers and consorts most had been murdered, and some were discovered barely alive having suffered great pains and torture at the hands of a rogue Klan of aliens known as the **Claw.**

The visiting scientific Nibiru team had buried the king under great Anunnaki ceremony having salvaged the lives of those who were left alive and with great care the saviours had nursed Anzu the alternative leader of the species back into good health. Anzu as the new evolving master would eventually take control of the planet on behalf of Lilith and over time the princess had made great sculptures in the King Alulu's honour for Anunnaki posterity whilst making a blood pact with the newly incumbent leader and thus, laid the seeds for her eventual return to take Queenship over the red planet.

Sitting within the scientific Anunnaki group were also a clutch of space travelling Igigi astronauts and a few highly advanced and very clever Pleiadian aliens comprising of twenty colonists and thirty-two female Anunnaki Nibirians who had accompanied the explorers on their star journey. The experts had already spent a considerable amount time on Mars eventually restructuring the new colony in its entirety. Although in the grander scheme of things the Anunnaki dominion legacy had left behind an effective Martian habitat commanded by a super dominant Anunnaki presence located within the dark-lands with a new **'Hive' outpost.**

The visitors eventually left the red planet albeit, Lilith was still harbouring the intention to return at a later time once the inception of the new colonial human hybrid **'seed'** on earth had taken place. After which she would then be ready to confront the disruptive Draco Claw species for out and out war and bring Anunnaki justice to those criminals who had murdered the Anunnaki King Alalu and claim the planet for the new Anunnaki.

Chapter One:

'The Beginning'

Definition of nexus: *Link or connection, the nexus between 'War and Peace'*
Anu Nexus: *Link between the Anunnaki and Humankind*

At a time when man toiled the vast deserts as ill-educated unevolved homo erecticus nomadic animals most likely during the early Mesolithic period there was an unusual shift within their surroundings when an armada of **space chariots** had arrived on earth from another galaxy, and as we understand it today these early visitors had settled in several ancient middle eastern countries to start their planned colonisation program. What really ensued thereafter was a rapid expansion and uncontrollable mixture of evolution coupled with the hyper development of a seed DNA program that would in simple terms accelerate the intellect of the humankind animal from neanderthal their current development stage, to a more educated, thinking and more socially responsible genome of human hybrid. It was intended that this new species would eventually learn and evolve as the main nexus between the humans and the Anunnaki species and over time would prove positive with extraordinary results where some of the colonies grew exponentially larger.

This was to be the intervention strategy of the Anunnaki legacy. A plan designed to form a workforce that could be initially controlled and one that would eventually become self-regulating under a human Pharaoh or King figure, simply in order to mine and procure the vast deposits of gold that lay begging to be extracted without the direct involvement of the Anunnaki actually being present in the country. Within the Anunnaki dominion legacy we have to touch on the subject matter of strict oversight command and control of humans, and to consider the course of what could be considered as intervention with the great floods or great deluge and other extremely violent catastrophic events that simply wiped-out mankind at some point in our existence. And these events were most likely a reality as the overlords had taken drastic measures to eradicate the rogue hybrid elements of their earlier project. Perhaps more than once whilst remaining cognisant and highly aware that such subject matter and the people concerned such as Enki, Enlil, EA, Inanna, Ishtar Noah, Thoth, Nimrod or even Gilgamesh commonly known as the Anunnaki 'Pantheon' may have been intertwined and ancient accounts reinvented for ease of understanding and perhaps history crosses several boundaries of understanding or acceptance regarding the Anunnaki endurance.

And as far as Sumerian history is concerned. Or conversely, as far as human evolution or their destruction is concerned. That may simply mean that some events could have been natural occurrences such as the demise of the polar ice caps for instance which had melted in times gone by and the sea levels simply raised to extraordinary levels and subsequently flooded the majority of the land mass across the planet, or perhaps the most difficult tablet to swallow is that a great Tsunami had erupted either after a nuclear explosion.

And most plausible of all that an unprecedented volcanic eruption had occurred on earth during antiquity. And, if we look deep enough, we will soon discover that human history does in fact repeat itself, more specifically as with the great biblical deluge. We may have to determine that two major events may have occurred, or was it just one event?

Two cataclysmic events which are remarkably very similar in context and may have even occurred many centuries apart. Or logically only **one event** was recorded twice as to keep the narrative alive. Of course, during all these wonderful epic tales and stories it will always be difficult to corroborate any such real truth around these occurrences especially, as they could have occurred several thousand years ago or more, and perhaps even before mankind as we know it was physically created. And subsequently, through the lineage and passage of time many important facts and important messages and accounts of world history may have been simply lost and crucial details mostly forgotten. Even more so, as the many Kings Queens and Warlords passed through their timeline on earth where we may discover the installation of deception and mis-direction stemming from the many narcissists including any alien species that wanted to be in charge of humanity and ultimately changed world history to suit their own ego's and their own corrupt volatile existence as they created a drive to rule the known globe and many Egyptian Pharaohs and their Queens being very good examples.

The Annunaki on the other hand as a species according to any good media search engine states that the powerful **space people** appear to have been on the planet earth for over half a million years or so, and they were most likely brought to the planet by their own overlords or the Elohim or Anakim for a special purpose. However, perhaps in the context of time and space terms that is probably not a long time at all for an intergalactic explorer on the search for important minerals or booty. Where intergalactic travel would be deemed a very short trip.

With this subject in mind and in human historical terms these ancient planet scientific explorers and investigators had certainly made a crucial impact on the planet's early inhabitants. Which in essence, is still a very strange notion for humankind back then or even today to fully comprehend. Perhaps, even now we cannot simply grasp the concept of aliens and their existence on our beautiful little planet as factual. Although many academics such Pliny, Plato, Plutarch, Socrates or Herodotus including Enoch in their time, who had as scholars all recorded many of the uncorroborated circumstances about the space people's arrival on the planet from other heavenly worlds arriving in their '**sky chariots**' and were perhaps more of a reality and not just a clutch of fabled conjecture or dreamy storytelling, but, was a real academic argument at the time where these great theologians and scholars were trying to rationalise the real reason why the early Anunnaki had chosen mother earth for their new beginnings.

Then again, we may also have to rely on many ancient writings such as the Enuma Elish and the Epic of Gilgamesh and many other obscure sources of information and determine what is fact and what is really fiction. And this task folks is by any means not an easy exercise to undertake. However, we should study the real reason for these visitations which could have been far more sinister in their concept and design during the early disruption within the cosmic grand plan or the mixing of the primordial soup pot than first anticipated, as described specifically under the Sumerian Enuma Elish (Origin of man) a fantastic account and storyline.

Perhaps the Anunnaki were seeking absolute planet domination and that these space explorers were in fact not only destined to plunder the planet's vast rich gold deposits which they could reduce into the elusive **manna gold** dust powder or **monoatomic** gold or the Pharaoh's **manna bread** for their own ends.

But were in essence here to create a new world order of beings and remained on earth for a few thousand years chiefly kicking off their new lives and quite simply began genetically re-engineering the human DNA to evolve the indigenous population as a human '**Slave**' workforce. A species that could eventually be **transported beyond that of the planet earth**, and a good reason for modern day alien abductions accounts that we know of.

However, dare we say that mankind was actually created by Gods for Gods and that we humankind should be eternally thankful for our existence, even though it was very clever and industrious master plan by the aliens to build an SS- **'Slave society'** under the watchful eyes of the early Anunnaki and the Igigi people in the first place.

Chapter Two:

'An Mer'

Introduction to An'Mer:

'I hate this planet, but, welcome to our post nuclear apocalyptic hell. They call me An'Mer well at least that's what my counterparts around here at the control centre call me, that name amongst many other names, I am sure. But in essence we are all Anunnaki child seeds who are surviving here in this closed habitat in the country known as Sinai on planet earth where we are constantly reminded by the elders of the Dominion that we are lucky to still be alive, especially after the great nuclear war with the '**Ender Race or the Draco**' had taken place. There after we were left alone not only to survive but also to be in command and control of the last remaining space port on the planet since the war erupted and the final destructive nuclear explosions had occurred. We are known within some Anunnaki echelons as the '**Lab test – Creatures**' or the breed that almost made the proverbial hybrid mark, and we despise this name tag as we collectively never made full hybrid status as our Anunnaki DNA bloods were far too strong and too potent to be genomed or fused together with the early incumbent mankind. Which as a result meant that we were given minor duties within the grander scheme of the Anunnaki construct. And therefore, we remained pure Anunnaki by default or perhaps by design. My own mother was said to be the infamous Princess Lilith of Nibiru and she was a very well educated Anunnaki space bio-scientist (genetic bio engineer) who had left our home planet to create the new humankind along with another bunch of biological specialists, but I should say that I have never actually met my maternal mother or as a minimum I really cannot remember her, nor have any other members of the colony. Nor can they recall meeting with any of their families, and for me especially with the enigma that seems to be attached to the entity known as Lilith. Although I should state at this juncture that it has been very quiet over the centuries since our arrival on this desolate planet. But, I do hear every now and then both wonderful and yet horrific things about her exploits on and off this world. And sadly, it's the same for most of the others here in this habitat who crave to be with their maternal families beyond this prison we call home.

As part of our existence, we do respond to the stories that we hear on the universal grapevine as they say. But in the early days we were all made outcasts from the very start of the implantation strategy, and we were somehow always destined to exist as an isolated colony. But after a short time, I changed all that, and I had taken control of the complex and broke the mind manipulating programming along with the four other warriors that I have here with me, and they are my brothers and sisters which I do regard them all as my direct family. As a collective group we are all trusted 'Merlithians' a name that we derived from the ancient Anunnaki anecdotes taken from the **hermetic wizards** and space travellers who changed the worlds they encountered by introducing technical wizardy and advanced sciences to less developed cultures across the cosmos and the planet Earth which was one such targeted planet and the name 'Mer'leen' appears in our texts as such a time traveller. Collectively, we are the so-called bastard children of the Anunnaki.

The last news I heard regarding the Princess Lilith was that she had left the earth colony and had ventured back to Nibiru after a great rift between the Royal high courts. And I understand that she was never in her own mind to be treated as a sub servient female to any male of the species apart from her trusted partner. And she had rebelled vigorously, and she either left the habitat by her own volition or was ousted. I really do not know which, but I understand my father may have also been the great Thoth, a theologian and biochemist and was renowned as a serpent king worshipper. A dominant male presence who provides me with a solid nexus and intellectual bloodline between myself and my ancient Anunnaki lineage. Which I can trace back to origin if true. Although, in my mind I still very much long to meet with Lilith and ask her many questions as to the Why? The Where? And the What? But more so to understand the reasoning behind why we had all been abandoned as Anunnaki children, or colloquially known also as those damned 'Nephs.' What I do recall however, was that not long after the Igigi expulsion or their exodus along with the Hyksos people out of the country around the same time as the great Santorini volcanic eruption had occurred which was followed by a range of devastating plagues and infestations then a palpable darkness of dense clouds laid across the skies of the middle east was when we realised that our existence was nearing an end.

Then, another disaster followed by the fallout from the volcanic eruptions that we have heard about even the news fell as far wide as Antarctica as an example. However, in this part of the world the Pharaoh and his colony across the lands of Egypt would have certainly blamed the sky gods for this intervention and somehow thought they themselves had upset the overlords in some way or fashion through their false idol worship of many icons within their polytheism or religious Egyptian ideology. But obviously, the ensuing conditions being the results from this cataclysmic volcanic activity several hundred kilometres away would have for certain changed the physical landscape beyond any recognition and introduced both the seismic underwater mantle shifts and tectonic plate disruptions creating perhaps a new continent. Which would have certainly caused the land mass to rise up creating great floods and tsunamis to occur.

And after all these natural events had settled down. We, then had to endure the warring efforts of the invading Draco species and the migration of the early Igigi workforce was when we actually fell into obscurity. Only connected to our kith and kin through the Pleiadian Skywatch team. What I can tell you as fact is that the original Nephilim children who were the designed hybrid race had once wreaked great havoc across the country in those early days, and they had quite literally created mayhem, chaos and unprecedented anarchy where we understand that these new breeds had also mated without fear with the evolving human woman-folk through their DNA blood program to such an extent, that the crossbreed colony had become an unhinged uncontrollable force and went against all the set parameters and guidelines laid down in the original Anunnaki plan. And thus, had to be extinguished rapidly for fear of overthrow of their masters. This mass cull was a direct result of their insidious depraved exploits and they were eventually albeit, unceremoniously removed from existence.

Whereupon, a new breed of mixed hybrids was soon to be created. The end-result of the first hybridisation program had failed miserably and had brought into existence a clutch of highly volatile, dangerous and maladjusted giant creatures who had rapidly evolved. Even down here at the Katerina habitat we had hid on many occasions from their volatile presence. Our own existence, however, was achieved by a strategy that took us higher into the mountain tops after the first deluge, and then the unannounced great war that had ensued leaving us once again very vulnerable. Where we as a small colony evolved at high altitude until the waters across the lands had subsided and dissipated sufficiently away, and then we had returned to the hidden caves at Katerina where luckily enough and we remained out of the reach of the nuclear attack. But were indeed lucky and managed to escape this great tragedy. Although in reality we had survived mainly due to the efforts of the Skywatch team and the arrival of the AIC - Ark Interception Craft, which the Pleiadians had sent to gather up the remaining key humans and of course the dominant Anunnaki leadership along with their vast library specimens of animal DNA to ensure that a full reconstruction of the planet could take place once the sands of time had settled.

In this instance we were tasked to remain behind. And we now know that the Pleiadians as a species can certainly be trusted as they are today. The old Anunnaki legacy and Nephilim culture has since been almost forgotten and through time has faded deeper into the recesses of our minds and we are the only true living survivors left behind here in Sinia to ensure that any final missions from beyond the planet earth can still be carried out by our progenitors. A secondary plan was also installed after the recent war with the Draco King which was a military strategy. And it was soon after the skies had been scorched by the nukes and the existence of the sulphurous volcanic dust that the Anunnaki along with the council of five had decided to close down the many space ports restricting any travel across all the colonies, and we find that only '**One**' other functional port can be safely activated today that we know of. And that is in a place called 'Antarctica' which is a very isolated and cold region on the planet where the Anunnaki and the remaining loyal Pleiadians (Arayans) and Igigi people now dwell in a safe haven called Ahgartha.

We have no physical craft here in Sinia to escape upon, but we do still provide direction and guidance to visiting craft, and we wait patiently to be rescued. Although by some strange recent events that have occurred at the Giza complex, we know that the control system in Egypt has been reactivated having been offline for nearly three thousand eight hundred and twelve earth years. Although at Katerina we don't really know why this has happened, but we do suspect that **human tomb** raiders or modern explorers may have found the last of the ancients such as King Gilgamesh and could have inadvertently closed or activated the Giza space gateway.

We do know that the gateways can only be opened and closed by Anunnaki directly, which has led us to think that these odd occurrences such as the retreat of the Draco species from planet earth may have also triggered a new beginning. And the opening of the space port is indicating or leading up to something quite biblical in proportion. But clearly to our thinking we know that there is Anunnaki involvement hidden somewhere deep within the threads of these events.

Which also means that we can potentially reboot and align the complete star systems back into normal operational status, and maybe then we the Anunnaki children can escape earth and return to our home planet of Nibiru. To this end however, here in Katerina I am also known as the go to person for any help or assistance to my colleagues as I am the oldest male of the species in the command centre team and our task as I have stated already was simply to control all craft movement across the many sky routes that serve the Anunnaki purpose. With this in mind the overlords have recently declared that two new controlled routes or fly zones are to be activated.

This action provides us with some hope that we are still in favour with our natural domain. The origins of my existence and that of my cohorts has always been somewhat vague in full memory to us all and is shrouded in certain uncertainty as have the remaining Igigi people who are our direct support crews who keep us in check and ensure that we have all the logistic support we need to conduct our daily business. But, let me tell you, it was not always this way, it was quite unorderly back then especially when the Draco had burnt the skies and slaughtered the inhabitants or attacked what was left to kill off from the species with their release of atomic weapons. And of course, the outer colonies had suffered exponentially as the Draco had dropped a littering of deadly nuclear fall-out dust over most of the land known within the Sodom and Gomorrah landscape, as they had executed previously on Mars. It was an event that almost wiped out the complete population along with our ground recon base staff. Today, as I experience the sights and sounds of our environment coupled with death's aromatic stench within our domain we can still taste the remnants of the mixed xenon, sulphur and salt gases loitering in the hot toxic atmosphere.

Myself, along with An'Chilles, An'Gregaar, An'Laara and An'Nanu are all that remain of the old colonial forces and we accept the fact that we may still have a greater role to play in the evolution of the Anunnaki master plan. Although we do still remind ourselves that it was during these wars that the early Nephilim prodigy children had stood by helpless and watched as the lands around them was burnt and scorched beyond all recognition and the people were consumed by the fires of hell. And, sadly, they too were eventually all wiped out. And for us lucky enough to still be alive, well these were our end days but, we were saved by the grace of our species and the great Enki entity and thus, we had survived.'

CHAPTER THREE:

'NIBIRU'

The planet of Nibiru is the eternal home of the ancient Anunnaki race of people, and since departing Earth's atmosphere the planet was continuing its long journey back across the stars with her three thousand six-hundred years orbital cycle around the cosmos and was recently navigating within the inner universe avoiding the cluster and mass of man-made satellites, telescopes and other technical space debris that lay in the planet's pathway. Albeit not really great hurdles to negotiate for this massive body. As the planet itself is approximately ten times the size of mother earth and orbits six hundred times farther around our known sun albeit in an anti-clockwise direction if general calculations are to be acknowledged. However, as this great mass was being propelled through the many star clusters of planets and had already left the magnetic pull of Earth far behind her and now! she was somehow still reported as being '**propelled**' along at great force by an unintroduced powerful 'push' that had affected all the heavenly bodies simultaneously. It was a cosmic interplanetary disruption and a great disturbance of immense magnitude which had obviously impacted other planets in its awesome destructive wake. And due to this unprecedented explosion, which simply caused the planets to be of out of both synchronicity and balance with their sister heavenly bodies, it was a real concern. And on reflection Nibiru has plunged deeper into the darkness of inner space.

From our knowledge and contact with our distant Pleaidian counterparts it appears that the planet 'Mars' had recently suffered another full-scale attack by a warring fraction and resulted in the spontaneous release of nuclear weapons at surface and that was creating this 'explosion' resulting in a massive electromagnetic pulse being shot across the universe equal to several hundreds of human styled atomic or hydrogen weapons being released at the same time into the inert atmosphere. We have also discovered recently that the Orion cluster had also momentarily shifted on its magnetic axis and was heading towards the sun by a mere few thousand celestial light years or so. But, the planet Nibiru was away off her normal track and was bound for a journey perhaps resulting in a no return orbit. The fear was that planet X could potentially not return on track and could become a future collision planet. This nucleic disruption in the cosmos raised huge concerns for all the other intergalactic colonies and the Anunnaki had realised that the remaining rogue species of an ancient 'Klan' under Shamgaz acting as their leader may have employed one of the last remaining ultra thermo-nuclear weapons of Armageddon that were taken off world by the ancient Anunnaki in years gone by.

This original ploy was an attempt to keep stability across the cosmos hence why the weapons were originally hidden near Mars in the first place. The weapons having been stored secretly in a subterranean chamber hive on the 'Phobos' a synthetic moon during the first voyage to Earth. It was deemed by the federation that the most likely cause of this explosion scenario was that the Draco Klan had in fact gained access to the ancient Anunnaki scientific war chest and destructive armoury, but they were still unsure about the status of the nuclear arsenal.

Shamgaz the **appointed one** had communicated his insidious deadly destructive intentions by releasing one of these test modules of - world killing weapons into the domain setting an example of what was to follow, especially if Shamgaz and his ludicrous demands were not met.

This release of weapons had sparked the start of another inter colonial war between many species across the universe which for all concerned would be disastrous. In essence, the cosmos as we understand it appeared to have suffered a huge magnetic glitch and had become misaligned as a result of this weapons deliberate planned release which also meant that all astral technologies and celestial travel data lines had been critically disrupted and would have to be rapidly updated and realigned in order to avoid any potential interstellar collision on a massive scale of magnitude towards WTF, and most likely involving the best part of nine planets across the known Milky Way, of which, the planets **Earth** or **Mars** could be considered as targets in the coming years.

Chapter Four:

'Lilith the Scientist'

In the centuries leading up to the great floods Lilith had primarily ventured to the planet earth with the Anunnaki as a scientist and her offspring would be the first planned DNA seed to start this new colony of servants, albeit, all was not perfect between Enki and Lilith and their co-existence was normally steeped in turmoil and very troublesome as they progressed the hybrid colony. Yet in her tenure Lilith had still spawned non-technical or natural children, although through the laboratory process these were mostly female, which excited Enki greatly as his love of the human creation remained intact but, as with natural feminine desire within pro-recreation and driven by her lust for unbridled sexual activity Lilith had also prevailed a hidden **'Seed'** a child secretly sown and was evolving in the backdrop within the mists of time.

And this was the bastard child of both **'Lilith'** and perhaps **Thoth**, and the entity evolved as a new breed Anunnaki warrior. Ancient mythical accounts will tell us that Lilith hails as a princess from the planet Nibiru as the disputed/undisputed key figure of our progenitors, who were in essence the star people known as the Dominion Anunnaki. The great Lilith however in her tenure had laid a trail of many names in her long existence such as: Ninti, Hathor, Isis, Ishtar, Athena and even Minerva depending on which part of the world one gains the details of this entity's life cycle from. But, by most standard accounts the Lilith was the daughter of the great **Anu** who was deemed the next Royal blood Kingship line to the Anunnaki Throne. According to history, Lilith having been expulsed from the great gardens of Eden was set on a new path of her evolution, it was an ethereal journey which was to become a travesty for the early Adamite humans and an endeavour that was never to support this new humankind – homo sapien breed nor their seed of creation as intended by the ancient Anunnaki visitors. Therefore, Lilith as a new lifeform had forged her way into the more deviant and obscure lands of the underworld of Hades. And time had ticked onwards designed for both Adam and the new Eve. However, their physical human sexual antics eventually had become too much even for the Lilith to endure and her anger finally erupted. The Anunnaki Princess had been so angry from day one, especially since the elders of the Anunnaki had also created the subservient Eve to accommodate the rapid retirement of Princess Lilith and then as a matter of pro-recreation she was quite unceremoniously banished and Lilith, man's 'First Lady' left the gardens for eternity, having been launched over the proverbial garden fence into the seedy and depraved world of the afterlife, so legend has it.

The Anunnaki princess had inadvertently become the devil's new advocate as she had been merely dismissed as a problem entirely out of hand and expunged for the advancement of the new Eve creation. The Lilith, therefore, had subsequently wandered the lands and skies in her nocturnal activity and then departed normality whilst ravaging the underworld on a campaign devouring all the offspring of lady Eve and any Adamite children coming into existence. Her destructive drive was in an effort to thwart mankind's planned evolution although from the onset the master plan was for her to actually nurture mankind as per Enki's ruling. It had become evident that the underworld of Hell had a new demon in their midst and like hell itself there was no fury so dangerous than a woman scorned and the Lilith was eventually unleashed on the human society and has returned to earth in the **twenty first** century.

Chapter Five:

'Overthrow'

Before her expulsion, Lilith formed part of the Anunnaki scientific group and had arrived on planet earth and decided to celebrate the life of King Alalu and had planted 'The Sacred Tree which was made from Nectar and was in reality to become better known as the *'Tree of life'* for immortality in memory of the King and she planted this wonderous iconic tree centrally within the great gardens of Eden. The real truth should it be known was that King Alula had actually been murdered or assassinated by the internal workings of the Anunnaki leadership under Anu directly who may have used the unwitting Draco Claw as part of his mass deception plan and had them murder Alalu, and probably is still a subject that is a matter for real debate.

It was an Anunnaki fact that Alalu had indeed in his destructive tenure nuked the planet earth and his attack on the marshy lands near Basra in Persia was to become part of his eventual downfall. His next unprecedent attack was toward the planet Niburu itself as another prime example with low level nuclear missiles which was the last straw for the Anunnaki to endure and the Anakim had taken clandestine steps to protect themselves from one of their own kind and Alalu was dealt with very swiftly. And all this decision making was executed in secret and unknown to the loyal princess Lilith at that time. As time passed by, the inhabitants of planet earth had evolved and Lilith eventually returned to Eden and had given birth to many more offspring albeit, (DNA laboratory manufactured) within the colony and she had also became locally known as the **fertile goddess** of creation. The princess of the stars was finally replaced by her namesake the entity **'Venus'**.

Although, Lilith during her earthly time had convinced Yahweh or Enlil the incumbent overlord of the earth miners to spare a segment of the new colony of hybrid humans especially during the times of the great deluge of at least thirteen thousand years ago and was a single strategy that she had engineered to protect her **hidden** offspring at San Katerina. But Lilith also had a master plan up her Anunnaki sleeve and she had hatched a secret domain in order to protect her hidden seed and evolution strategy for a new colony.

As the human hybrids settled themselves on earth Yahweh was eventually selected to govern over both the Igigi people and the hybrid colony for many centuries to follow. In the years that had passed by, Princess Lilith had also built several palaces of Anunnaki worship across many countries for her early dominion rule. But, over time it was the more dominative Queen 'Ninmah' that had evolved and ruled alongside her brothers Enki and Enlil in the country of Sinia under the Queen's stricter rule.

In Lilith's devious mind however Mars was still on her long-term radar and agenda to over-rule where she had learned a great deal more about these destructive advanced weapon systems and she had gained the technical know-how that was at her at her fingertips that could threaten the very stability of the universe, and she could potentially eradicate any single planet especially with a wide range of strategic warheads that were secreted in the underground chamber only known to the Anunnaki as **'The Hive.'** And of course, Lilith saw this as an ideal option for potential overthrow and create her own domination legacy using this planet killing technology as her weapons of choice.

Unlike the Draco, the Princess was more super-devious and she would strike fast and hard in order to negotiate a complete Martian overthrow and rule the planet with absolute authority but, she also knew that this strategy would certainly quickly alienate her from her many cohorts and colleagues. But she also understood that she would have to engage and defeat the new emerging Martian Klan that had already attempted to destroy the Anunnaki presence on the planet by attacking what they thought was the hive location. This was determined in great contemplation by the overlords as to the why this early attack had occurred and the Klan had released one of the lower technical level destructive weapons at surface as a sign of their potential power. Lilith, then drew on the one **'Force'** she knew that could remove and defeat the Klan (Claw) from existence whilst ensuring for the time being that she could also restore peace and harmony on the red planet until her dominion plan could be fully actioned, and subsequently she had released her 'hidden seed' the **Merlithian.**

Chapter Six:

'The Seed – An'Mer'

'The Merlithian'

In the far-off lands within the country of Sinia obscured in a dessert location near to the great mountain range a single remote location known as the – 'Ra' Katerina Caves' there is an Anunnaki settlement that had been established millenia ago. The structure was built into the rock face before the great deluge had wiped the lands clean of the early DNA creation and had from that point onwards the lands remained a desolate and inhospitable barren desert for quite some time. The Merlithian as they call themselves had been formed from a small powerful enclave of mixed Anunnaki children whilst working under the auspice of being planned Nephilim hybrid humans, which would become part of the **'Golden slave train'**, but who were in essence secret Anunnaki offspring and were flourishing as a small colony within the expansive landscape. The habitat – Ra'Katerina at Ararat and was originally built by the first Anunnaki settlers under the auspice as a safe retreat in case their own expulsion from the planet earth would have to be executed and therefore, secretly maintained this outpost accordingly. This was the earthly domain of the first designated Anunnaki children and within this colony there existed only five giants and several watchers of which, a few were non-hybrid humans amongst them. There is one powerful Anunnaki male seed who had evolved as their commander and this leader was 'The bastard child of Lilith known as – **'An'Mer'**. This warrior stood at seven foot four inches tall and was a muscle-bound monster of a beast, who was strong fearless and wise which made him a very dangerous adversary indeed. His pseudo family are also tall and the two Anunnaki women amongst them may have reached heights of six to seven feet and were also built strong, but unlike the menfolk the women were great thinkers as opposed to the men being the hunter gatherers of their clan. An'Mer's duties were to support spaceport operations along the 30th parallel and to ensure that the landing corridors for any Anunnaki craft movement were aligned between Giza, Sinia- Tilmun at Moriah, Lebanon and the planet Nibiru and ensured that all was in order to control the powerful locating beacons, communication pods and that they functioned correctly and that the command structure complex remained powered up and fully active at all times. This was achieved whilst operating through their central mission control outpost known as the Tripex.

The main Tripex powerhouse and control centre for operations back then was originally located in the deserts of Egypt at Giza at 'The Sphinx complex' which also housed an accommodation hub and the power sources for the main frame computing systems. Giza was deemed the final landing port for visitors to and from earth and Baalbek in Lebanon was for VIP's and heavier cargo craft. The landing zone at Giza marked the Southwest line that had originally started at Mount Ararat in Turkey and was just located at a junction between the Northeast runway conversion leading on to the approach gate. Sinai on the other hand was primarily considered as the main runway entrance corridor and Lebanon was the initial transit route and rendezvous point of entry for the Igigi people specifically, but the overall control was reassigned after the proverbial dust had settled in Sinai after the great nucleic turmoil.

And the Tripex at Giza was duly closed down. Each location known in this modern day would be recognisable as having pyramid styled structures that housed the technology for space travel, and were pretty much replicated in their design, shape and style across the many countries within the seven continents. These pyramid structures were dispersed at strategic points that ran along the full concentric edge of the planet Earth whilst traversing the ever-pulsing magnetic Telluric ley lines running under the planet's rocky surface.

An'Mer acting as the commander basically oversaw the movement of the interstellar craft within Earth's domain and communicated directly with Sky-watch (sky chamber) a remote Pleiadian manned station near to Orion's belt that was deemed the eyes of the cosmos and basically regulated craft movement outside earth's boundaries whilst also maintaining a secondary mission control observation platform called 'Cylink'. This was a military outpost and interception station that was designed to keep invading entities clear of the sky routes to and from the Pleiadies, Mars, Nibiru, Orion and of course Earth. The rationale for the constant oversight by the Pleiadians, was designed to thwart any future potential release of nuclear or hydrogenic weapons in the 'Minerva and Andromeda belts' which could potentially shut down both travel and the communications link networks across the central universe. The base worked on a strategy for the early engagement of unannounced or hostile craft on positive identification which was highly important. Any outlaw entities or smugglers would be attacked and most likely destroyed. But we understand today that the Draco species had already managed to deceive the outpost guards and had circumnavigated a space pathway with one of their craft and landed directly on the Mars surface and pretty much started a colonial war.

Today amongst very ancient warnings we observe, is that the highly acclaimed Sumerian cuneiform clay tablets and early writings from countries such as Babylon, Mesopotamia, and Sumeria amongst other locations are examples that tell us of an **'ancient war'** and details are mirrored or captured within the biblical book of Genesis and if, we refer to certain Christian bible writings which do allude somewhat to highlighting destructive weapons being released on the planet at some point in time. And scarily enough recent archaeological discoveries of **radio-active material discovered in** ancient human skeletal remains may indicate or can corroborate the stories of ancient nuclear war or nuclear activity to a reasonable degree of understanding, or these human bodies had been involved in extreme volcanic events mainly due to the presence of 'xenon' gases discovered in the calcium (boned) body clocks and could be taken literally as fact that perhaps the release of ancient nuclear weapons in antiquity may have led to the demise of the evolving Sumerian people or the early hybrid program. Although since the nuclear attack on the planet, most of the space ports had been shut down and they had remained so until very recent times.

Chapter Seven:

'Mars'

The Hive:

The hive structure located on the planet Mars is a very large complex that sits subsurface on the far edge of the Eastern Dark-lands and was designed to keep control of many ancient Anunnaki technologies that today modern mankind would find as high-end state of the art technology and full of concepts of which 'should' be beyond their human comprehension. The main underground complex itself has four points of entry:

One entry point in this structure quadrant which is manned (droned) by a troop of synthetic security drones who patrol the fifteen kilometres long boundaries at surface ensuring that only approved visitors could enter the complex especially the 'Magazine' area that housed the advanced weaponry systems and the bio - laboratories, including a battery of the remaining nuclear Anunnaki Armageddon warheads.

The second part of the hive complex is the data gathering centre where all the neuro electrical programming and synthetic intellectual systems are housed. The finished product being the brain which would then be installed as designed into the alien Artillery pieces. After which the god killing intelligent weapons would be ready for testing.

The third segment of this unique habitat is the physical assembly plant where the full main missile assemblage and multi control surfaces and main computer installation for final construction would take place and made ready before they could be moved, re-tested or installed into a transport craft or attack craft for mobilisation purposes.

The fourth section of the complex is the domestic hub of the habitat and was the sleeping pod compound which is annexed to the core complex and run from a central globe structure that could be raised above surface and lowered as and when required and housed at least fifty-eight Martian scientists and their Anunnaki colleagues supported closely by the Igigi people.

The main control structure by all accounts can be lowered to at least 1200 metres below surface if required to evade any attacking craft or to escape the extreme weather temperatures. At each corner of the complex stands a single one hundred, forty-foot high obelisk reaching into the darkness of space, these are the location beacons and each tower is topped off by a large golden rebroadcast pyramid or similar Ben Ben stone, an apex module that emits skywave ultra-high frequency signals to ensure that travel across the cosmos was controlled and the communications systems remained functional. These huge monoliths could also be lowered or raised when required. The Hive had been constructed many thousands of years before the decision was made to travel to the planet earth, and the red planet Mars was a key staging post for the Anunnaki to travel within the universe and were using the planet and it's engineered moon '**Phobos**' as a resting station coupled with an equipment repair workshop.

In many ways the planet Mars is very similar to that of Earth with water, clouds, winds and also appears to have a twenty-four-hour, daily time cycle. The environment shows many strange weather patterns including its effect on the polar ice caps, which is perhaps whilst on earth the Anunnaki fled to Antarctica from Egypt after the great Hyksos exodus in order to escape the revolutionary mankind and the rogue Igigi people who had evolved beyond their design.

Where we may find in reality, the humans had become a troublesome creature to command and control as were the developing Igigi people. The terrain on Mars, such as mountains, rivers, lakes etc make the planet pretty much a second home for the Anunnaki and resembled Nibiru in many ways, hence, probably why it was first choice of planet before adventuring onwards to planet earth for their exploitation of the minerals program, as Mars was close enough and was the perfect staging post.

The planet also suffers extreme hot and cold weather spells as does earth and temperatures range from about minus sixty- two degrees and much lower in the winter cycles and conversely the extreme heat can rise to plus ninety degrees in the summer months. The red planet as man understands it through time immemorial was always dubbed a warring planet if records and history were to be believed, and the ancient Babylonian astronomers and astrologers would have known this planet as '**Nergal**' sadly, the planet is pretty much associated with both pestilence and war.

Chapter Eight:

'Mum's the Word'

An'Mer had sat down near to the control panel of the electronic guidance system and shook his head slowly from side to side, he was a little worried about his state of mind but not too disturbed in the sense that he was in any danger, well not as yet anyway as he gazed upon his forearm once again and acknowledged that the marks on his limbs must have come from somewhere? Perhaps through a bump or a knock or maybe it's just older bruising he had not recognised, but he was thinking something else, it looked almost like a tattoo inscription if so, then how could it suddenly appear from nowhere on a person without any intervention or event that he could remember. Then of course, there were also the recent hallucinations that had been hounding and haunting him over the last few nights and was being kept awake through his disrupted dreams. But as a strong leader he thought to himself it really wasn't the time to talk to anyone in the colony just yet about his condition just in case he had suffered from some strange bio-chemical exposure or had reacted with the earthly gases that were once released during the earlier nuclear war. And any recent exposure may have simply irritated his skin. But, as he rubbed the area around the blemish marks he thought that he could actually make out a few letters, and if asked he would say that this mark looked very much like Anunnaki script within the bruising and he then held his arm up to the light. An'Mer remained very aware that they had not had any direct contact with the planet Nibiru or the early colony settlers for such a long time and they never really expected to be rescued either after so much time, hence, why they evolved the colony in the first place and for centuries there had been no direct communication with the Anunnaki outpost apart from one or two interventions handled through the Pleaidians a few months ago. Maybe because he was core Anunnaki that he was just over thinking his situation and thought that an initial Anunnaki contact could have been activated. And this was a certain dream for freedom for any prisoner to acknowledge. He then decided that he was going to wait until he could talk directly with An'Laara his partner about such strange things especially as the women of the Anunnaki species were far more advanced in their perception and logical thinking. It was by design captured within the feminine intellectual make up as they were almost pure psychic in nature than that of the male across the species.

An'Laara, as a person was more adept and very much in tune with the world of contact tattoos and such blood line inscriptions and their very obscure meanings, but, what An'Mer himself could only deduce was that this was either an early warning sign or that he was somehow ill, or it was really a calling. And as yet he was still unsure what it was one hundred percent as the Anunnaki communicated in many strange and wonderous ways? Well, for now what these markings were was still anyone's guess. But his own thinking was, that this sign had something to do with his maternal mother 'Lilith' and she could have sent an awakening call in the medium of a sign in her motherly common DNA bond. The DNA bond being an Anunnaki process that only the mother blood line can initiate and basically sends a genome calling card no less with the word *'Lilith'* being accompanied with a small **Ankh** insignia, both denoting contact, and in Anunnaki terms that would be the first contact sign.

An'Mer thought for a few more seconds about his state of health again then left the command console and searched for his partner within the habitat complex, eventually finding her immersed whilst enjoying her daily dip in the 'deep pool' or the ritual mud mineral bath, which was in essence a heated mud filled pond that was laced with many crystals and healing qualities.

The 'goo' in the mud bath was saturated with off world minerals and various salts and chemicals that sustained the skin tone of the species. He waited and watched for a few moments then disturbed the peace and tranquility of the spa. 'An'Laara, I need your help, what do you understand from this Anunnaki contact mark? look! I have skin markings?' At first, I thought they were just bruises, but now, I think this has come directly from Lilith. But I am not sure what it really means?' An'Laara stared at the markings for a few seconds before commenting, then took a single globed shaped pocket of iced alcohol from a decanter and consumed it quickly. It was the proverbial Anunnaki drinks cabinet or pocket decanter resembling more of a bunch of glass grapes hanging on a hooked hanger than anything else, then she responded. 'It's a contact tag sure enough. This could be a direct command to find Lilith and a request to join her in whatever endeavour she has in mind for you. It looks like to me that it is your time to leave Katerina. It's definitely a primary Anunnaki marker, I am sure of that, and you may have to embark on your destined journey of life. Oh, for the heavens in harmony, you are so very lucky, but, what about us? Are we to be left behind? Will we have to remain here unless of course, there is also a cause for us to follow on.' An'Laara

'The Seed': 'Anu – Nexus'

appeared sad at first and her feminine intuitive mind wandered in and out of reality as she tried to find the rationale behind this unannounced calling from Lilith. Her psyche had gone into deep over-load and she began tapping into the universal vibrational frequencies of the deeper cosmos when, she suddenly placed both hands on her forehead. 'Wait! let me think about this for a minute or two.' There was a moment's pause and a very awkward period of silence ensued as An'Laara contemplated the information about her companion being summoned to join the distant Anunnaki colony. Which also meant that he would be taken from her and their Merlithian colony. As An'Mer and An' Laara spoke for a while longer a few other blemishes had appeared on both of An'Mer's fore arms. And it looked as if Lilith was certainly calling not only her boy but the full Anunnaki conclave from the Katerina colony. Which meant it was not just An'Mer receiving this calling from Lilith, but it appeared she was summoning the other group members as well through their maternal blood lines, comprising of the five initial hybrid children. Of course, in the modern context the Merlithian were not minor figures anymore either, but were a full blood mature breed of Anunnaki people. An'Laara gazed upon her own forearm and spied a similar mark that had started to appear. 'Look!' she cried out.' Whilst raising her arms into the air and watched eagerly as the sheen of yellow gloop globules dripped down from her limbs exposing the clear lettering of the word 'Lilith', then she spoke in a very excited tone. 'We are all being summoned look, this is incredibly amazing, maybe we can leave this habitat together forever. But, I really think we are all going home.' An'Laara appeared even more excited and started splashing about in the 'goo' again as if nothing else in her life mattered. An'Mer smiled as he watched on, because in reality the Anunnaki never seemed to smile, their eyes would often soften and the pupils would fully dilate when intrigued or bemused by something that triggered their sense of belonging, but a nice smug smirk had appeared on his face as he watched on. An'Laara almost smiled back at him then spoke.

'If this is real then we can all go together to meet our families, but we will not leave a single Merlithian behind. We all have to go together or not at all, it's the Anunnaki way, because I really do feel and think that something must be terribly wrong in the annexed colony if they are summoning our help in this way. Although in reality, they could have just sent a craft to pick us all up, I also feel maybe Lilith has another master plan for us all to undertake.' An'Mer nodded in agreement. 'Yes, that's what I was thinking, but what? As I am also wondering An'Laara as to how Lilith can call us all in this collective manner as this for me is a common mother blood bond?' An 'Laara, smiled and clicked her fingers a few times in the air then responded. 'The Anunnaki are ubiquitous we are all connected through our DNA, often we can feel pain and pleasure as a collective albeit, sometimes we don't, and I have to agree with you that only Mothers can call the Anunnaki children of the species, although the great question to ask is? 'Are we all Lilith's offspring.' And without any doubt these markings indicate that all our families are still alive and must be congregated somewhere, most likely here on earth, **Ahgartha** would be my best guess.'

CHAPTER NINE:

'BOXED CRIMINALS'

The American military strike team had strategically entered the tomb at surface and were steadily making their way down through the dark cavern to the lowest and probably the darkest chamber of the secluded chasm, it was soon after entry that the commander gave the sudden command to his soldiers to halt. Something had caught his eye. For a moment or two the Sergeant was a little apprehensive perhaps a tad nervous and thought that he had seen movement at the far end of the chamber and had cocked his Armalite M16 assault weapon by instinct ensuring that any sudden attack on the team would be instantly met and thwarted with a volley of machine gun fire. But then again maybe it was just the shadows that were playing games with his vision, which was fairly common whilst underground. He then took a deep breath and contacted his superior at operations echelon via the hand-held radio. 'Halo, Bravo Three Alpha, this is Sandhawk we have secured location Alpha November Uniform One, area and all seems quiet, it appears we have multiple artefacts in place, over.' The Sergeant then waited patiently for a response and tasked his team to remain vigilant and take secure cover in case they were attacked. Then the response call came. 'Sandhawk this is 'Sandy Central (HB3A), proceed with extreme caution you have clearance to capture or destroy over.' The Sergeant then responded. 'Central we have three large sarcophagi easily excess of ten metric tons each, four small Ossuaries, fifteen alabaster or granite cases and twelve large glass jars, request helicopter extraction soonest, over.' The response came back very quickly. 'Roger that, extraction will be in twenty-one minutes clear landing zone for helo pick up, send coordinates, out!

The final military expedition in Iraq in early 2000 may have concluded with the custody of ancient famous key historical figure bodies as examples and could be such alien beings as Enki, Gilgamesh/Nimrod or indeed other great Kings and Queens who have laid in waiting over thousands of years pending their re-animation by the Anunnaki. But this uncontrolled intervention by an alien command such as the American military humans was not intended. Humans had not learned from the nineteen sixty-one (1961), exploration and had forgotten about the early ISIS program that removing ancient bodies from their eternal resting places had severe consequences and was never going to be good news. We are reminded when the Russians and the Chinese had rocked the cradle of alien harmony a range of inexplicable events had struck their country and was simply played down by the host government. This American intervention however had triggered a sensitive relationship with the space people but the recent repeat of such events were not to be taken lightly and the Anunnaki were watching closely as mankind disturbed the various interplanetary species from their graves or hibernation chambers. The Anunnaki slumber period having been interrupted by the US Military forces in Iraq and the powers that be who dwelled in the heavens were not exactly impressed. This act would be seen by the Anunnaki overlords as being a direct wage of war against the Anunnaki themselves, and not just with the American armed forces either. But with humanity in general. And now the United States and other countries in their true blind arrogance, ignorance and lack of moral compass coupled with their disdain and absolute disrespect for other life species will certainly suffer for their haphazard attempts at raising the mighty Gods of history. But in essence, they may have also just signed the death warrant for mankind for their actions. The attack on Iraq also witnessed the removal of all articles of interest by the yanks as they plundered the many museums across the country and had acted on the finer details from an archaeological dig from several months earlier which, according to some military and political rogue journalists had really sparked the Iraqi war which was then to be the **undisclosed** excuse to obtain these alien artefacts.

With such history and archaeological finds many researchers may have aligned Osiris and Gilgamesh or indeed Nimrod together, but with Nimrod as a rogue alien we have to tread very carefully, as Nimrod was certainly not a nice character either. His legacy of existence was steeped in hellish activity and may have been sent on a great task by the overlords to root out those kings and leaders who would not conform to the Anunnaki grand plan. And he this great warrior subsequently invaded many countries and destroyed many cities and removed many Kings in the process. We could of course think or determine that Nimrod was an **alien internal political terrorist** who in reality, followed his Anunnaki godhead and rules. But he was also a thinker who would instil in man the desire to fight for their own beliefs and build a super race that required loose alignment to the Anunnaki plan.

In history Nimrod has a very bad almost evil press having set forth from Kush his home country and both rejuvenated and destroyed many monarchies in his wake. The king had set a standard that may have also driven tyrants through history such as Ghengis Khan, Pohl Pott and Hitler in their future's in their unrelenting barbaric signature footprint for attacking humans. Nimrod would, therefore, eventually drive a belief towards the elements of **Earth, Wind and Fire** and thus, presented the natural world to man against some other alien beliefs. Nimrod would then fall into historical obscurity and fall out of grace as a tyrant hunter of **men** and not animals as a hunter gatherer. Albeit, some biblical researchers reckon that these beings such as Gilgamesh and Nimrod as a tyrant could be one of the same entity or even their next generation offspring. And were then interred at various time frames across our human timeline and would have certainly walked amongst men and women in their lives on the planet. And they had certainly influenced mankind greatly to achieve great discoveries. Nimrod without question was also a great magician, tactician or he was a highly advanced being who had taken charge of engineering mankind's DNA. And now today without question we witness his prodigy or alien genome offspring seeking his vast knowledge with what can only be described as for military advancement. We also must remain mindful that not just Nimrod but, all of these alien entities were predators, unlike some of our visitors who were of a benign or good nature and displayed great empathy towards humankind as was Enki and the Pleaidians. Therefore, again we must allude to the Anunnaki presence on earth and their enduring existence which had also been tarnished with credit to great bouts of bloodshed, war, pestilence and unprecedented representations of demonology. It is by fair assumption that the great Nimrod may have been the **Chief demon maker** himself and was certainly aligned to Princess Lilith in their thinking and their early concerted efforts to create and control the children of the eternal Anunnaki over eight thousand years ago was fact. However, as an example the aliens were a primary hunter gatherer species and Nimrod may have been tasked with a very significant force in the evolution of human history. But, it still remains to be seen as to what extent the gods were satisfied with his monumental efforts with humans, and still remains to be seen as the library of over twenty thousand plus cunieform scripts reveal their true story.

Mankind in this modern age may well still be at the mercy of his eternal wrath as the **cross-breeding** experiments continue. But, as a very stark warning to the American military, NATO and other countries, is that any efforts to disturb any of these great entities or others at this time, would be both suicidal and the undoing of mankind yet again. Unless of course the Americans had unearthed an entity that was **not** Nimrod **nor** any of his clan and that would mean utter chaos and more mass human bloodshed would ensue. It is with foresight that we should determine whether the intentions of the Americans or the Russians was actually to create a new breed of blood seeking vampires and monsters which was still unclear currently and perhaps, why? we have no real solid eye-witness accounts of these ancient hybrid beasties roaming the lands or suburban areas of our major cities. Or conversely, the creations could still be in suspended animation within the uncontrolled breeding program initiated by the Igigi and the Draco together at the DARPA scientific secret laboratories. In the grander scheme of things the Anunnaki have also determined that the alien hybrids will stop at nothing in order to overthrow the Anunnaki species and have specifically set the wheels of control in motion to ensure that they repel the Draco Claw, and if that also meant awakening the Gods to intervene, then the Gods 'shall' be disturbed and they probably will not be too happy about it. We should remind mankind that these alien species stood at eight foot in height minimum and had reached to around fourteen foot in height for advanced Nephilim in ancient days, and the sad reality is that mankind are already trying to destroy the very creation that might have created them in the first place. According to the legend of the Ankh within the known original cipher text or hidden codex of Enki, it states that reprisal for any war against the **Anunnaki** will be met with the instant removal of mankind and any species that dares to interrupt the great Anunnaki master plan which basically implies, that they will be harshly dealt with. Today, in the twenty first century the Anunnaki have almost certainly returned to the planet earth and walk amongst us but not as giants or strange creatures, but as an integrative species who can shapeshift to accommodate their existence in their own likeness to modern mankind, and they are about to remove a range of select world leaders and their corrupt governments in a few swift highly technical moves. For this strategy a general assembly was being planned for world leaders to unite in harmony and fight against the world's poverty crisis and ironically. If the truth were revealed that these greedy world leaders and law makers had also knowingly created this mess in the first place then, they were about to be held accountable. The aim of the assembly was to bring together a political body or force that could reduce illness, famin, drought and death to the global masses. Albeit, unknown to many of these elite classes their time on this planet was almost up. The Anunnaki **purple blood line** classes were about to be removed from the face of the earth, for their eternal, greed, war, pestilence and murder of hundreds of thousands of innocent people that they were destined and supposed to protect. The twenty first century will witness a new beginning as the crowns of the worlds start to die off like flies infesting a putrid deceased carcass of the **'Heavenly body'** that they have unreservedly ravaged and devoured, and the Anunnaki target was the body of intellectual modern man and they, this elite insidious class had selfishly evolved a murderous military slave force to do their unworldly deeds. The summit or the gathering of the **'Elite'** was planned before the end of the year providing that the Anunnaki can both stop the Draco in their take-over bid whilst ensuring that the great Gods are available to witness the **'Wholesale slaughter'** of yet another failed program in their human construct. But this slaughter was to be silent, swift and very painful, unlike the drastic destruction of the land mass and the use of nuclear weapons technology that would take an evolution to clean up and recover from. However, in good standing and terrible order, the welcome package that was despatched to the world's elite royal households was by virtue and the introduction of a few high-end trinkets and chocolates provided from the Middle Eastern world as a token of trade and value. The female jewellery was exceptional in quality and Carl Faberge' himself would have been impressed, the ladies received a long gold and platinum necklace chain with a central, green, emerald jewel piece that sparkled in any light. And this was no ordinary jewel, however, this was a rare **'Death's Eyedrop' gem**.

The Anunnaki had ensured that the gem was perfect in every way possible, and that the expensive box of chocolates that accompanied it was laced with the 'Antagen' that would trigger the desired response. The menfolk on the other hand had also received a unique finger ring of gold and an emerald stone with an inscription welcoming them in the world's elite's big boys club. And of course, accompanied with a box of the finest cigars also laced with a coating of the killer 'Antagen'.

According to the Anunnaki users guide manual. This was the cleanest and most efficient method to employ. Should all else fail, then the animal hybrid blood antigen programs were going to become a back-up plan. Which meant direct contact and physical intervention, and attention was drawn to the Basque enclave that serves the early centre of antigen manipulation and captures this rare **'R' Type bloodline** of the true Enki lineage, and the Anunnaki must be protected at all costs, but the 'human cull' could still potentially fail. But then again the Anunnaki had been decisive and executed their plan as designed with no flaws.

Chapter Ten:

'Breakout'

DARPA Holding cells:

The American and Science biological testing labs at Lake Edge, near Groom Lake Nevada, at the DARPA site had made a major scientific breakthrough with their Franken Bio program having taken an advanced leap in nanugenetics and had successfully cross pollinated a modern human gene with a supposed donor from an ancient so-called Anunnaki sample seed. It was a sample taken from the DNA of an ancient warrior that was discovered in ancient Mesopotamia in early two thousand and five by the American military. However, it appeared back then that medical ethics, social responsibility and basic good will and intention had been dramatically overlooked by the American Military along with a 'knot' of deranged scientists who were still attempting to create a super-breed of hybrid human warriors. The drive behind this madcap initiative being that the military wanted a one-man killing machine or a group that was impervious to biological chemical attacks and would stand against a wide range of small arms weaponry. Weapons normally designed to incapacitate soldiers as opposed to killing them outright. The rationale behind this logic was simple logistics being that it took three men per casualty to assist in rescue and recovery within the battle theatre, where battlefield resources would be quickly eaten up and depleted leaving a void of teeth arms to fight onwards without real boots on the ground. This new seed would be the ultimate killing entity and the Americans wanted to be the first to develop alien DNA into their warrior military arsenal, albeit, these were never going to be normal warriors by any stretch of the imagination? These samples were considered as pure ancient breed aliens within an advanced genotype of bloods that any scientist or academic scholar would never understand their molecular structure, let alone try and tamper with it successfully. The warning being that **rogue DNA** from non-Anunnaki specimens would create an uncontrollable monster from an alien hell and would be dangerous during any stage of its creation and development. Which is why the project was deemed a practical disaster by some of the high-ranking Military critics from the onset. The only unforeseen problem was that the actual rate of growth for this experiment was exponentially rapid and the creature evolved nine to ten times faster than mankind had anticipated since the early collaboration of the Chinese and American ISIS DNA trials.

This evolution frightened the scientists greatly and they tried to stem their prodigy from evolving as quickly as it was, but, alas it was to no avail. The military machine could not stop the program and nor did it wish to, and the politicians simply kept pumping funding into several projects under the star-spangled banner. Therefore, it was not too long after the ISIS hybrid was born that the 'abomination' was physically walking the earth within a few short years. Although this mutation, this new age beast creation had recently **escaped** confinement and was reported to be lurking somewhere deep in the Nevada desert and was feeding off the land. The earlier research program in the late 50's was well underway when many scientists could not agree on the practical aspects for the road ahead and were dismissed by the military or they had simply gone missing, but in stark reality the act of altering the genetic sequence coding of any animal at this time seemed to have driven a very large unethical stake through the hearts and minds of the good solid and loyal academics. Conversely, some of the lesser conscientious scientists only saw the high dollar signs dangling in front of their noses and the insidious **reptile of greed** raised its ugly brow and reaped the benefits of military logic along with the proceeds from the American public purse.

Whilst others saw the dangers and had removed themselves from DARPA projects completely and were swiftly alienated, silenced and removed from such projects as operation 'Skin-Tight' and were banned from any further involvement in DARPA's activities. The mindset being that these scientists essentially did not want to be party to the worst case of medical intervention plausible. It was with hindsight that DARPA also evolved its activities into human mind manipulation and had commenced many projects that would unleash a science that would potentially control the minds of certain humans and the 'Matrix' theory was soon born. The military logic on the other hand was simply designing weapons to kill or control fellow man. Even more so as the yanks craved superior military dominance across the globe and understood that any scientific breakthrough was generally treated with open arms. The DNA in breeding program as an example was originally dispelled by some of the academic community that the notion of cross mixing breeds would never be a reality. However, the underground **'alien integration programs'** as was project **skin-tight** was working under an alien known as **J-2-Jo** and others within DARPA and they continued uninterrupted, nevertheless. The USA along with many other governments were already attempting to clone a multitude of mixed species together. And now! the military appear to have the blessing of a rogue alien entity. And the result was supposedly wandering the Nevada desert attacking and potentially eating its away across America.

The real problem was that the beast was moving at an incredible speed and the armed forces struggled to keep the alien on their proverbial radar. Washington was already deeply concerned and had sent a crack team of combat marines deep into the Nevada desert on a seek and destroy mission. The real political angle was that the United States could not be seen to have lost control of any one of their planned 'projects' but, things were far worse than they had first anticipated and the loose breed may have moved on too swiftly for the yanks to keep control. All was not lost however as the alien synthetic forces through the Pleiadians at Skylink themselves had intercepted several radio communications and had contacted the Antarctica base for their direct support. The Watchers at 'habitat one' had engaged with the Pleiadian strike team and they had activated the secret hybrid colony at Sinai and the Merlithian through an alien being known as Lilith and she had already responded. At the DARPA installation however, all was not perfect either and the Americans had indeed recovered some sarcophagi and other ancient alien artefacts from their warring exploits overseas but what they did not know nor really understand was that the newly discovered hibernating bodies **were not** the great entities such as Nimrod or Gilgamesh but in fact were a **Clutch** of the last remaining incendiary criminal elements of Draco lizard breeds known as the **Claw (the serpent worshippers)** on the planet which were in essence a trio or group of killers that were hell bent in ousting the Anunnaki forever. This Homo Nephillim hybrid was a clear example of mis-direction by the Draco Claw leadership whilst working under a new technology at DARPA and this was that their rogue DNA program which had been secretly installed into the human breeding syllabus and was administered with the external assistance from alien bio-scientists armed with the technical biotechnical know how and scope of ultra **'hybridization'** techniques concerning the human make up. And the revenge program towards the Anunnaki was not that far from becoming a reality and was certainly within human or as a minimum Draco reach. Sitting behind the backdrop of deception was the Klan's leader Shamgaz and he was hellbent and intent on creating hybrid warriors working within the human test labs in order to try and destroy the core Anunnaki at source.

And, furthermore, in order to provide a kernel of thought to the reader. If indeed the Egyptian Archaeologists as an example had indeed discovered the final resting place of Osiris near the Chefren pyramid or the great Sphinx located some thirty metres below surface. Then many questions must be asked for assurances purposes as to what has happened to the remains of these sleeping giant's or their hibernating bodies? (if they were recovered) and were any real-time DNA samples extracted from them? and where are they now? When reviewing the letters of the archaeologists we will find that what they were describing in their initial findings was indeed interesting but, what? was physically discovered within the chamber is not clear. Was it an entity or just the sarcophagus itself or was it a being that was not of the human realm or simply a run of the mill Pharoah interred as expected. And was it really a single central sarcophagus sitting between four pillars emersed in water, or was this something else? But, who? On the other hand, was the unidentified entity that was also supposedly found in **Iraq, was it a similar being perhaps,** which was discovered then removed and the opportunity taken by unscrupulous governments to find and relocate this great ancient warrior for cross **breeding programs**. Which could only be a certain disaster for mankind if these tomb robbers have dabbled in sciences they do not fully comprehend. And this perseverance and line of direction will ultimately lead to their eventual destruction via the biblical anti-christ figure in the form of a **Draco lizard** entity. A beast that will be permitted free reign over the planet earth. Such an event as prophesised by the **Apostle Paul** in the early days explains this very subject which is clear enough, whilst simultaneously, the great prophet **I**saiah son of **Amos** also prophesised the return of these **alien beings** who will destroy Babylon, but not just Babylon in this case. But most of the other existing colonies across the planet. Although the prophet **Isaiah** himself would never have anticipated any unannounced resurrection of the overlords let alone, consider the third destruction of earth as was Sodom and Gomorrah, which may have only been a **nuclear test bed** example, for alien learning purposes. But modern humans should remain hyper sceptical and be alerted that the American and Russian Military along with the Chinese will be dealt an **unearthly strike** from the Anunnaki in retaliation for their actions as a revisit to the human race ensues to determine their physical removal from earth once again. It will be a swift clean strike that would surely rain down more fire and brimstone in the form of a nuclear attack for disturbing these great beasts of history. Or something else. Perhaps a modern-day epidemic or great plague such as a Covid virus especially as the Administrations of presidents Bush and the senate or Yeltsin and the Polit bureau or the Chinese Government as clear examples had allegedly been caught with their fingers in the political corruption pies, having already removed many relics **not** of this world from the museums in and around Iraq and the other middle eastern provinces. And had, specifically dug up the interred slumbering giants.

Enoch stated in his revelations the location as to where the true antediluvian Nephilim lay and were probably still interred there at this location. Perhaps we now know that they may have moved or had been disturbed at some point in time. **Enoch** himself may have been a human that was taken to the stars or was abducted as have many others may have been. Most notably Admiral Richard Byrd in the modern day. And they the sleeping demons may have relocated and interred themselves to safer havens in the remotest of countries of Antarctica, Norway or Scotland and were making preparation to reset their '**seeds**' of both law and order and the natural course of events whilst keeping mankind in check. Or the worst case of all, were they planning to take revenge as they have done so, over many centuries by inflicting their wrath on mankind.

Chapter Eleven:

'Darpa'

Defence Advanced Research Projects Agency:

The DARPA annex base commander Lt Col Edmund Khan located at test facilities Groom Lake zone 3A, had just reached over to pick up his mobile phone when a single sharp lizard talon was thrust deep into the top of his left hand. The creature suddenly emerging from the shadows had pinned the appendage of the soldier to the heavy oak desk without any warning. 'Arrrgh.! Cried the officer as he tried to struggle with the beast that had skewered him. As Khan looked up and stared into the evil green eyes of the invading alien he then took a single large deep breath of air of which, was probably his last whilst realising that any fight for freedom with his unannounced alien visitor was going to be nothing but futile. The beast towered over him at seven foot in height and yet moved slowly and silently. Then the creature spoke. 'You really should not do that earthling, we cannot permit people like yourself to tell everyone beyond this domain that we are awake, and we know that you have already leaked memos to your command. You must realise that you and your humankind are an ignorant species and yet you still manage to rock the delicate balance within the human cradle of life. You have no comprehension in what you have already done as a species, and you sit there not yet knowing that the ancient Nephilim have been resurrected and will destroy your complete breed and remove them as we do any toxic virus in existence. But sadly, for you, it is time for you to leave this physical plain.' Just then another larger slimed talon met with the soft skin of the commander's neckline and pierced his throat in one slashing strike leaving a six-inch long incision running from one ear to the other across the commander's jawline. It was a clean surgical laceration almost medically applied but nevertheless, the whip of the talon almost severed the head of the base commander in a single fatal blow. After a few bodily gargles and slurps the limp body fell forward spilling blood in all directions across the antique oak desktop. Then what was left of the base commander slithered out of the round backed chair and clumped down on to the floor of his office. As the hybrid creature moved around the office space it then stopped and glanced over the computer screen of the ex-commander and quizzed the display. An electronic secret document sat open on the desktop appearing to explain about the interests of DARPA and the potential cloning of multi species, with the extract highlighting several warnings about continuing with any ad hoc future experiments. The author of the document questioned the ethics of conducting hybrid programs that would lead to human arrogance about reviving ancient DNA across many species and argued that man was not ready to play God with any sub species.

The creature smirked then muttered a few syllables. 'Humans, they are getting wise and perhaps a little too more evolved.' Then the creature left the office space. The new watchers however were already on the warpath and had been alerted to DARPA's un-regulated scientific programs and knew that someone within the establishment had already engaged with external forces. Where the decision was made to find a solution to seek and destroy this clutch of rogue Claw hybrids. Albeit, the Draco species had anticipated this move and began resurrecting the remaining two other sleeping giants, pending the arrival of their leader Shamgaz. The notion of war on earth with the Draco was being considered at the highest alien command levels. And the inevitable outcome would mean that only bloodshed would ensue no matter which way the proverbial onion was sliced, but the Anunnaki will not be deterred.

The plan was simply to send primary Anunnaki to deal with new hybrid Nephilim, and, as prophesised by **Enoch** who wrote about the deceased offspring of the watchers and the giants Nephilim, actually being resurrected in future time on the planet as they were currently concealed together somewhere in secret hibernation habitat hives, that were strewn across planet and were destined to have a new encounter to the death.

Book of Enoch:15:8-10

Now the giants, who have been born in spirit, and of flesh, shall be called upon earth evil spirits. And of earth shall be their habitation. Evil spirits shall proceed from their flesh, because they were created from above. From the holy Watchers was their beginning and primary foundation. Evil spirits shall they be upon earth, and the spirits of the wicked shall they be called. The habitation of the spirits from heaven, but upon earth shall be the habitation of terrestrial spirits. Who are born on earth.

Enoch may have had access to time travel or was channelling and saw glimpses of the future and the impending intergalactic species at war on earth.

But the question as to how he really knew and received this information would perhaps never be answered in our lifetime. His resources of information may have stemmed from off world and most likely if true will never be released in their entirety to the human population at large. And yet another *ancient prophecy* may have already be coming into play.

The United States of America had just kicked off a potential new world war with an off-world species that they could never win. The real anarchist and deadly alien spirits having been evoked as they had been in times past, albeit back then the space people had emerged on earth just before the time of the great floods of circa BC 2500 to 2300 and were simply seen as perhaps aggressive. Or they had as a minimum planned the great flood to wipe the slate clean of their failed human genesis project or was this due to a cataclysmic event that could have been triggered by a striking comet hitting the planet or indeed a massive Tsunami coming in from the Indian ocean. Again, we must ask ourselves? was this due to nuclear war? And had these entities been forewarned of pending encounters and they themselves had migrated their hibernation program to far off lands. And are they planning to return?

Respected academics may agree that a planned holocaust via a collision from an asteroid was perceived to hit the earth in 2012, and in essence should have occurred in that year, but this event passed without any collision or any global demise or any worrying events. The Anunnaki secret records may state that the Anunnaki were indeed disturbed in their underground safe havens by the Americans or others. And perhaps not for the first time either. Such movement and engagement with the aliens may have actually averted their potential demise as it was determined in history circa 2012, that a planned strike will bring down the **fires of hell** was a **fact** and elements of the Anunnaki Dominion had already been alerted and were resurrected and the course of these so-called **prophetic events** were dealt with by unknown alien intervention at that time to keep a certain harmony. And, after their interventions soon found safer havens as a precautionary measure.

All that remained to be understood in this modern day was that the real **chariots of fire, flying carpets or flying shields** as first recorded in antiquity were not just ancient stories, myths and legends reported by many cultures, but were in fact no different as to what we observe and report today as modern-day high end technically advanced flying or underwater craft UFO or UAO/USO's are being reported. And craft that are being witnessed in the skies by the hundreds if not thousands of sightings annually across the oceans and many countries in times past and present. And remember folks that the language skills of ancient civilizations were not advanced enough to discuss or describe **flying technology in any great detail** and therefore, local myths and cave drawings coupled with early descriptions are as much relevant today as they were back then. The stark warning for humanity is that the Anunnaki will return and set the records straight. As it is clearly evident that they have never lost sight of the human race and their ill development. But new, repercussions will unfold as the Anunnaki take revenge on the political loose cannons and the greed of the monarchies who have permitted the disturbance of these sleeping giants to take place. And the modern grave robbers and their leadership of both civil or military regimes will also suffer as had recent military leaders.

If the Iraqi country invasion was indeed the catalyst for deception in recovering alien artifacts out of modern Babylon. Then we should stand back and watch as each world leader is surgically removed from society by the Anunnaki scientific construct starting with the yanks. But even more so as other alien species start to occupy our planet and oust the incumbent watchers and perhaps in the longer term bring even greater havoc to mankind. Then we must make no assumptions that the Draco Claw are not weak and are a force to treat with ultimate caution. These are the new Nephilim and we should all be frightened as they will simply penetrate humanity and wreak havoc across the planet and remove elements of mankind that simply do not fit the proverbial social integration alien bill. And we will undoubtedly fall back into a horrendous life of servitude, unless we are wiped out completely by yet another nuclear atomic war.

Chapter Twelve:

'Antartica'

The Habitat and colony outpost at Ahgartha was relatively quiet and the human workforce along with the multiple project teams had continued to conduct their science work at surface nearer to the McMurdo base station and remained quite oblivious to what was really evolving three miles deep under the mass of ice. The trusted watchers had already assembled their teams and were making ready to relocate from their outpost and begin preparations in moving towards the country of Sinai in the eastern deserts accompanied by the Pleiadians on their new mission. The plan was to engage first with the Merlithian at the Katerina outpost then bring the five Anunnaki pure breeds back to Antarctica as directed by Lilith where the early generation could interface directly with their natural Anunnaki family at habitat One (Antarctica).

Kemp Hastings, Darlene Gammay and Erica Vine had all evolved in both intellect and their human appearance since remaining in Antarctica amongst the Anunnaki after the overthrow of the Draco Serpent King -The Draaken several years back. And the girls had become emotionally healthier and had been taught the advanced ways of the Pleiadian people. Kemp Hastings in his own emotional state of intelligence was calmer and at great peace with himself. Although he flirted with the same human mindset as previously as an eternal sceptic but, he had changed greatly in his rationale thinking towards his perception of aliens in general having remained unconvinced about their primary existence for quite some time. That was of course up until his direct encounter with the great Nimrod and Lilith in what seemed like only yesterday, and all his reservations, conjecture and thoughts had faded away into obscurity. He was now more intellectually aware of his journey in life as his mind had also been enhanced. And the best part of all was the opening of his proverbial **pineal eye** (gland) which was awake. His physical body although still muscle toned had become slightly larger in muscle structure as his Anunnaki bloodline had taken root whilst dwelling in his new domain along with Anu's clan and his diet which was certainly strange in nature and not really normal for a man to actually consume copious amounts of such strange fish and other beasties of the seas, albeit, Hastings was indeed the last DNA strain of real human hybrid lineage of the ancient Anunnaki.

His hair was not as long but was certainly whiter and he pretty much resembled the ancient human figure known as the biblical Noah if he was to be honest with himself, but he was quite comfortable with his appearance especially since the Pleiadians had triggered his DNA upgrades. The Anunnaki had a new watcher in their presence and Hastings was about to embark on a journey that would lead him and his colleagues into an unknown and a highly charged political war with both a mixed colony of human military and some advanced nasty rogue aliens, let alone being introduced to several 'Plains of vibrational travel' or 'out of body excursions' designed to meet in the spheres of the afterlife. The worst part of all was that the International Governments knew what troubles were brewing regarding secret alien programs most of the time, and yet they had not raised a finger of suspicion towards the USA, China or the Russians for fear of reprisal, then of course one has to assume that the world leaders are in league with one another and are quite literally being controlled by an unknown or undisclosed ancient alien force.

Chapter Thirteen:

'God's Deadly Garden'

Erica Vine the Arcturian was traversing the nurtured gardens of her nursery when she realised that none of the animals like the spiders, snakes and other little verminy dudes would cross the threshold into her inner sanctum. And she watched with great interest as the lizards, spiders and mice all crawled slowly pass the doorway then sprinted off into the glass annexed atrium which was located adjacent. Then, the creatures would scurry off out of sight. This spectacular display of hiding and seek was in the Ahgartha atrium that consisted of the more exotic plant and flora life that had been engineered in the Habitat over centuries. But Erica had created this project based on her research by her own understanding of alien myths and legends. And she grew and harvested hundreds of some very old and highly interesting but highly toxic plants indeed. She would say that **'garlic'** was a good condiment for any really tasty meal and had planted several bulbs at the east end of the greenhouse. She also knew that this was the **ultimate vegetable** for repelling snakes and lizards due to its potent aromatic fragrance which was highly offensive to some species and yet very acceptable for others. But as far as snakes were concerned they **hated** this plant with a passion as the oils contained within the stem actually made their snake skin dry out rapidly, creating acute irritation and surface skin boils would appear as the sap took a grip on its host. Which in Anunnaki terms is the opposing idea of existence as the primary Anunnaki bloodline could have well derived from the **dragons (snake) blood** elixir of life.

As Erica moved through the greenhouse she stopped and caressed the long soft stem of the **Serpentina** plant of which, the roots and foliage contain a very bitter citrus or lemon sap and contained a chemical that snakes certainly do not want to know or even be nearby to this humble innocent looking little plant. The understanding was that the **'reserpine'** component of the flower actually slows down the heart rate of the animal and the snake displays signs of tense anxiety and will make all haste to evade the somewhat benign plant. Erica had observed this trait all too often and knew that if she could harness the citrus and garlic oils together in greater quantity then she would have a chance at poisoning the Draco lizards if need be. Thus, very easily achieved by creating a spray repellent so toxic that they would not have to undergo any real face to face conflict with the Claw.

After a few minutes Hastings had entered the Atrium and started looking around the vast array of green things he could not recognise let alone name, it was his first visit to his colleague in many days. 'I see you are harnessing mother nature's little green children then.' Erica smiled back at him then responded. 'Yep it relaxes me, I feel as though I am protecting these little fellas from that horrible big wide nasty universe out there. But you know what Kemp there is a wee experiment that I have been conducting, I have actually identified twelve plants that actually do repel snakes, lizards, rats and other creatures. It is quite amazing, look here, if you look around the greenhouse floors and corner recesses you will observe that these places are free of any rodents and all the other little critters that should be naturally here, well, to be honest they have all exited this part of the garden and gone next door into the **sweet** plant room, where I planted rows upon rows of honeysuckle and sycamore plants just after our arrival. Now, I firmly believe that these plants have their own toxic natural defence systems, and if we can gather enough of these mixed oils and saps together then we can potentially saturate the Draco with them and render them pretty much useless if, and when we encounter them.'

Hastings tapped the garlic plant. 'Yep, don't much care for garlic myself but if you recall that we had dropped gallons of this shit on the Draaken King and his Army not so long back, but I fear, it was really the white phosphorous chemical that did the actual trick. But you may just have stumbled on something very interesting there, as I know absolutely nothing about such plants, unless the three I think I know a little about, which are the Marigold and the Mother In Laws tongue which is fairly obvious in question.' He added in humorous gesture. 'And the amazing Andrographis Paniculata, but, not really sure how many more I could name. But if they were all in one single volatile compound, then Erica you may be quite correct in the potential of using this serpentine mix as a real deterrent rather than a direct weapon. But we could pave or create a path of sorts leading the Draco Claw into an actual enclosed zone by spreading the sap in heavy layers in key places. And luring them first with your sweet honeysuckle syrup then melt them with your Lizard Elixir of Demise, what do you think of that? See if you can make up a couple of litres of your **'anti snake potion'** and we will try an experiment.' Erica agreed then opened her laptop and wrote a few notes:

'The Seed': 'Anu – Nexus'

Serpents connect with venom and medicine. *The spit of the snake or its venom is associated with certain plants and fungi, therefore logic dictates that for an event where snake poison is injected or absorbed into the skin then, as an antidote it can overcome the effects of the bite. Furthermore, certain plants and oils can be highly hallucinogenic and can expand conscious thought. The term of divine intoxication brings the user into a higher conscious state and can induce trances if ingested. The result being a 'trip' whilst taking subjects to another level in the cosmic vibrational matrix. Can we drug the Draco and get them high as the proverbial kite before we attack them.*

Erica then gazed on the embossed figure in the paper block text on the document and huffed a little to herself. The effigy printed on the page was holding the staff of life with a single snake wrapped around its entire length. 'Aaaaah! She then sighed. 'The Staff of Aaron, no wonder they have designs on taking the stone keys and tablets from Axum.' Just then Darlene had entered the garden Habitat. 'What you up to girl?' She politely Asked. As Erica brushed the hair from her brow then responded. 'Wow it is getting busy in here, two visits in one day, glad you came, I am working out some heavy-duty plant life drugs and hallucinogens to attack the Draco with, And, by the way you have just missed Kemp he is off to find An'Mer. I think he said that they are not quite sure how to deal with these weapons that the aliens say are hidden here at the Ahgartha magazine complex. And perhaps more up there in space land. It looks as if they might have been moved or relocated.' Darlene, then smiled and answered back. 'It stands to bloody reason that if the Draco have already released such a weapon on the surface of Mars, then logic says they might have acquired the complete bunch of bullets.' Erica shook her head in agreement. 'Yep, that is a real possibility, I think they call them a **battery** as a collection of guns, rockets, or a silo pod, one of the two, anyway you know what I mean, just like chickens living in a coup all huddled together.' She then laughed to herself. 'Imagine the irony of asking the Draco the question of evolution and what came first **'the snake or the snake's egg'** they would simply melt down with such a conundrum.' Darlene smiled and commented before leaving the atrium.'You need to keep yourself away from those hallucinogenic plants and drugs Erica they are screwing with your mind, you are starting to sound more like Hastings every day.' Erica smiled. 'Well, if you don't know, then, you don't know.' Darlene turned slowly and left the Greenhouse. 'Catch ya later.' She shouted as she slid the atrium door to one side and waved.

Chapter Fourteen:

'Arrival'

The Pleiadian craft had arrived at Antarctica with the five Merlithian on board and had eventually assembled at Habitat One and yet thirty minutes earlier they were at the Sinia outpost Ra' Katerina in the desert waiting for pick up. The outpost which had once been bustling with activity was now currently manned only by a skeleton crew of Igigi people that were to guide the craft beyond the planet Earth if, and when required. An'Mer the leader of his strike team had met with his maternal mother the great Lilith and the others with their lost families. An'mer himself had spent less than fifteen minutes with the Anunnaki Princess and all the history and questions regarding his long enduring existence had been laid to rest. However, on introduction to Kemp Hastings An'Mer was not so convinced that the humans could be of any real help, and could not quite conceive the fact that a mere human in the twenty first century could be in any way turn out to be his natural blood line relative either, given that Hastings was smaller and appeared too smooth and introvert to be pure Anunnaki and thus, An'Mer had questioned Lilith. 'How can a mere human be a match in power and intellect as the Anunnaki? This being will surely be a hindrance to our quest, and his consorts the Pleiadian and the Arcturian what can they bring to this war. Remember we are dealing with rogue Draco Claw. These humans will be slaughtered within seconds, surely. Mother it would be wise to leave them to journey their own life here at Habitat One. I ask you mother of the heavens to reconsider this plan.' Lilith went very quiet and paced slowly around the chamber a couple of times before making any further comment, she appeared to be displaced by the direct line of questioning or challenge from her son and then took several glances back at him before responding. 'An'Mer, the human Hastings has the concept of advanced human military warfare and strategy, and above all the human logic in his mind, he possesses an element of cunning and dare I say, that he certainly does not think like Anunnaki, but he is highly unpredictable and brave as any Anunnaki warrior I have observed. And remember he had engaged the Draco King one on one during their attack here on earth and this human won a battle that no other human would dare to undertake against all the known odds, let alone survive. Right now, there have been disruptions across the solar system and I am informed that the Draco are on the warpath, we cannot take any chances and we must use our resources and act swiftly. The Draco do not know how to read humans as we do, therefore he must form part of the strike team here on earth, and on Mars if need be. I command that you support his every effort and you will listen to his advice and guidance whilst also listening to that of the other human watchers. They are all hybrid breeds and as a collective they are strong, dangerous and highly resourceful and carry the support of the outer colonies.

The Draco will underestimate their power or impact potential, and this has already been proven. Once we take Mars and setup our new domain the humans will return here to earth and continue on their journey. But only when we are through dealing with the Draco, then you are to remain on the red planet until my arrival and together we shall re-establish the outer moon complex - 'Phobos' and build a strategic second base where we can run the Mars Hive from using a remote command centre, as we once did. Remember my child these are not ancient times and many species have greatly evolved. And we the Anunnaki are somewhat vulnerable until we re-establish the colonies on Mars, Orion and Earth. Your father Thoth would have never approved of this quest, and that is why? I have chosen you and the Merlithian to take direct control from the Draco. You are not known to them yet, nor do they know of the human existence within our midst, and trust me this has been the Anunnaki plan all along.'

There was a moments pause and then An'Mer sighed as Lilith continued. 'What I do understand is that there are three known rogue Draco 'Claws' currently on the loose and are roaming the lands of the Americas or are located at this laboratory in the desert, you must go find them hunt them down and destroy them all, leaving no trace of DNA samples for the humans ever to progress again. Once you have completed this task then infiltrate the political infrastructure of the human establishment at this place called DARPA and this is where the human hybrids will help you gain access. The current Igigi people at this establishment presently are too close to the humans and have guided them to create these rogue Nephilim monsters. And they must also be stopped and punished in their tracks and destroyed without question. As they are also to be held responsible for the Draco's desire to take over planet earth and that of Mars. Once you arrive on Mars, you can locate the Hive where you will find three weapons that remain and they must be secured. It may be wise to destroy the hive after you recover the weapons and then build a new complex on the south side of the planet deep into the wastelands. This An'Mer are my demands. Do you have anything further you wish to say.'

An'Mer bowed his head and bent down on to one knee. Lilith walked closely by him and placed her left hand on the crown of his head. 'This is your calling, my son, demonstrate your power and wisdom and let the Merlithian know that this is my desire. One last thing I do wish that the Princess An'Laara to remain with me here in Antarctica. As I need her womb and your seed as she is already spawning. We have our future colony to think about. Now go in peace and do my willing.' An'Mer reached out and grabbed the hand of Lilith and spoke softly. 'Mother of the heavens your wishes are my commands, rest assured that I will do as you desire.' Lilith smiled. 'Good boy, mother knows best.'

Chapter Fifteen:

'An Gregaar'

'The ICE chariot – Go Globes'

An'Mer had summoned the chief Engineer An 'Gregaar to the habitat hub. 'An'Gregaar I need your help? We are to transit across the snow plain in order to meet the Pleiadian craft nearer the oceans edge and from there on to San Katerina Ararat by air. Although we must bring the three humans with us. The vehicles must be able to glide over the ice fields, like the sand ones they use on Orion and powered by magnetism, if possible, constructed of both mercury and liquid titan steel. We cannot fly all the way from here as the Draco will know that a craft will have left Ahgartha giving away one of our exit points, and we will be shot down like flies being swatted on the chest of a pharaoh, if we are not careful. I need the craft to be silent and swift but with sufficient room to house our (unarmoured) bodies for four Anunnaki beings as Lilith has decreed that An'Laara will remain here, but you will obviously join us, I know it is not an easy task considering that we the legacy Anunnaki people are over seven foot in height. But once we shed our armour, we should be less tall, but! We will be vulnerable my friend, it is a risk that we need to take. I am also aware that we will resemble a group of shining greys as we travel, and An'Nanu herself will have to endure the light and intense heat as will the humans.' An'Gregaar stroked his forehead then spoke.'Yep, that can be achieved but remember that An'Nanu is chameleonic and that our females can change skin tone, sadly we males cannot. Do you think shedding our armour is necessary? We will need it, because we cannot go up against the Claw without heavy armour. That course of action will leave ourselves open and vulnerable to any physical assault outside the 'go globes', I can design the inners to keep us safe and we will be protected from earth's many viruses, but the craft internally would be made of a composite living mesh tissue providing a very robust and suitable protection for our skin, and also for breathing purposes. The frame should be able to protect us from any potential collision effects.' An' Gregaar then gave much thought to the request and had agreed to construct the 'go globes' to house both Anunnaki and the human team for their journey across the Tundra. This was a short-term measure until such times as the strike team could transfer to the lighter Pleiadian Ark Assault Craft and venture onwards to the lands of the Americas via air, thus remaining unnoticed whilst evading the scrutiny of the **interstellar radar.** Where the Draco Claw regime had employed **Sci Trak technology** to track and trace airborne movements across the magnetic 30th parallel. And most likely outbound of Antarctica. This was a military soft strategy or stage one, based on the fact that the Merlithian knew only too well that any above surface magnetic squeeze of more than twenty feet above the Telluric ley lines would be instantly detected and signify a presence or an electronic signature, however **'slight'** it may be. An'Mer sort of smiled. 'I know but we will need a bio suit, maybe we can store the armour somewhere in the human pod.' An'Gregaar almost smiled. 'It is so good to be amongst our people, even for a short time. So, tell me An'Mer where are we going first?' He asked in anticipation. A response came. 'We will eventually meet in Egypt somewhere near Abydos, one of the old Pleiadian birthing chambers, but we need to get back to San Katerina first, apparently there is an active gate that is still functional at Hathor. Lilith has decreed that we must engage with the law lords through the 4th Dimensional gate, and that is where we go '*vibrational*' to meet the council.'

An'Gregaar responded with an excited tone. 'Things must be really critical if they are going to open the 'vibes' to access the great and the good so, I reckon it must be at the 'Hathor' Temple it is the only zeta gateway that I know of that may still be operating and, that is, if it still works.' An'Mer took a deep breath. 'Most Likely, I do agree, but we will have to go back to Ararat first, as we need some of the tech gear you made and need to ensure that we can face the Claw with all the resources we have available.

The Anunnaki master plan under Lilith and her strategy, that is to be our primary guideline. And then after Katerina we embark on our critical mission to DARPA in Nevada. The Claw have somehow taken over the military complex and have setup their headquarters in preparation for an attack on the remaining outposts.' The stealth visit to the 30th Parallel should ensure that An'Mer and the Merlithian team could assemble their own batch of technical weapons and take actions and precautions to sever or disrupt the magnetic data lines and any contact media to and from **Giza to the American desert** for a short period of time. Or at least long enough for disrupting and preventing any space craft to operate or function normally. And the Claw would be literally radar blind for a considerable amount of time.'

As Kemp Hastings mulled over his predicament, he had also concluded that Darlene Gammay and Erica Vine had certainly changed since their relocation to Antarctica a few years back and were all working in harmony with the Igigi people and other ice dwellers where, they had melded together with their respective primal origin star species of the Pleiadians and Arcturians and of course the core Anunnaki. The Pleiadians themselves were presently the hub or core operators in maintaining the balance of Habitat life and pretty much managed all the mundane aspects and activities with great ease and precision. The Arcturians on the other were the thinkers of the colony and provided deep insight on bio life and the management of the wide array of aquatic species that roamed the vast waters around the continent. Although in the course of time and after his own valient efforts to save the great Nimrod and his Queen consort from certain death, the human Kemp Hastings had been elevated to the rank of **Imperial Protector** and was tasked to ensure that the Anunnaki would never be vulnerable ever again to any external attack at least from the humans. For this role he was given a protective Ankh with staff and the tree of life wristwatch or bracelet as his private indicators of both power and standing within the colony. Hastings and the girls were for all intents and purposes the new human protectors of the greatest entities dwelling or at least slumbering on the planet earth. The Anunnaki.

Chapter Sixteen:

'The Covenant of the Anunnaki'

Kemp Hastings sat quietly in the domestic hive at Ahgartha and was contemplating the plan to deal with the rogue Draco that were wreaking havoc some seven thousand miles away in the Americas when he was disturbed by the sound of soft footsteps coming from behind him. He turned slowly and was confronted by the presence of the beautiful An'Laara. She had stopped a few feet away and stared for a few seconds directly at him. Hastings was a bit surprised and felt quite uneasy not only by her tall stature but also by her elegant beauty, he had thought that for a very tall woman she was quite alluring, almost sexy if he was being honest with himself. He stood up and waited for a few more moments. Then An'Laara spoke. 'You are the one they call Hastings, the human warrior I hear so much about, the human who defeated the Draco King. Well, I should say that's not an easy task battling with a Draco King figure at any-time let alone surviving.' Hastings smiled and responded in kind. 'I was not alone at that time, I had help from the Princess Lilith and the great new reborn Nimrod who were there by my side. But I think they had really done all the hard work, I merely captured the Draaken by placing the Ankh around his neck, rendering him pretty much useless, and the powers of the Anunnaki did the rest.' An' Laara tilted her head to one side almost smiling for the second time in as many hours then she retorted. 'Modest as well as intelligent, I am An' Laara one of the Merlithian family and not so! mister Hastings or should I say 'Anu Hastings' Imperial Protector. It is an honour having wielded the great Ankh which is in itself a feat that most Anunnaki male beings can only dream about in their own wildest of dreams. And yet you have also witnessed its awesome power used in **'anger'** first hand, and prevented a violent revolution from taking place and halted the potential violent slaughter of the human race as we saw it.' Hastings took another deep breath whilst dwelling on the events of the past Draco encounter, which was an event almost ending his own life, then he posed a question. 'Tell, me An'Laara, I know that the female Anunnaki are highly intuitive, can you tell me, what is this third covenant I hear so much about, and why? is it so important to the Draco? I am aware of the Holy Ark

'The Seed': 'Anu – Nexus'

of the covenant here on earth but, I have never heard of any other covenants such as this.' An'Laara clasped her hands together then decided to provide some oversight as how the Anunnaki bond with other races is balanced using the decree of the covenant. She then sat down and gazed over Hastings as she talked. 'The Anunnaki covenant is not exactly a simple agreement per se but is more of a common bond by granting the protection of a very valuable gemstone or tablet. The real jewel or tablet itself is one of the hardest diamonds in existence. But this one relic in its completeness has ancient supernatural vibrational properties having its origins hailing from the middle of the red sun. And that fact makes this shiny stone quite unique indeed. It is a power source that must be housed in a golden casket or heavy-duty containment shell and the stone itself remains eternally radio-active and seems to purr as the gem particles are exposed to radio activity or when excited by magnetism and although they appear as a flat styled tablets when moved from their caskets, they are actually, oval and bevelled in shape. But they are still just a bed of pure energy. They remain like this until the vibrations settle back down and become a sold mass. The Star stones can and do randomly regenerate power fluxes using earth's magnetic fields in this case. But do not be deceived by their size or shape. These covenant tablets must be treated with the ultimate safety precautions in place. The jewel in the state of '**power up mode**' was only to be used by the Anunnaki scientists for technical reasons.

It seems that on earth it is a treasure that humans would never fully understand and they were gifted with two tablets to protect. The relic you know of today hails from Nibiru our home planet, it is the source that also drives the time networks across the universe, (**known as the keys of Nergal**) and it is the ultimate Anunnaki 'clock.' The relic comprises of nine segments and each unit provides exact locations by species and their craft movements with entry points in and out of **time and space and of course their designated planet,** then places them all into specific astral corridors that infiltrate the vastness of the heavens. But these location points are never in the same place twice, unless of course you can understand the key's actual make up, or have the ability to calibrate the device to your own ends. And this is something that not even the core Anunnaki fully understand. But to answer your question. It is a covenant bond between the heavenly species and serves great purpose. And for the Anunnaki of Nibiru the **key** serves to align and harmonise our key planets of Nibiru, Earth,Mars and the full constellation of Orion together. But, please remember that the energy cells also contain the activation sequence codes to '**arm or disarm**' certain celestial nucleic weapons. And on Mars such weapons do exist.'

Hastings was lost in what he thought was an amazing revelation that would rock any religious belief across the planet then listened as the Anunnaki lady spoke. 'Tell me Anu 'Hastings why do you ask this strange question?' Hastings nodded his head and then thought about an appropriate answer. 'Well, I can only presume that what we call the Ark of the Covenant here on earth is such a segment or off world **tablet piece** taken from this great icon you call the Star stone. (Keys of Nergal) But, can they really be used control humankind today by mind manipulation?' An'Laara took a long sigh then answered. 'In one word NO, it is the overlords who protect the relic that spreads their intentions through religious doctrine and war, remember, mortal man is kept in fear of the unknown and that is quite frightening. You humans you are so inquisitive and caught up in your unrelenting thirst for knowledge, this is quite a unique trait, because most other species just want and crave the protective cover of the key itself. But you humans, you want to strip it down to the very core DNA of the relic and see how it ticks. Of course, this is an admirable quality. However, it is a trend that will see many evolutions of mankind's demise as the leaders try to control their flock. If it does not go unchecked. I should also say to you that you are indeed correct in your understanding that this earthly bound Ark indeed houses pieces of the Nergal construct, and of which there are nine segments of the Anunnaki **'Star Stone'** or the great power train. But this icon also serves as a reminder to humankind that this 'Talisman' is still a powerful deadly weapon and possesses a great power source that keeps the many stargates functioning. Although here on earth it is a nothing more than a very powerful nuclear density capacitor or reactor, which is highly dangerous. And can in certain conditions **spit** out bolts of highly charged electronic pulses from the container shell when it is disturbed or is placed directly over a charged magnetic source. In the old days the humans were provided with only two keys. **One** key to maintain the location of the jewel but, nothing more. The overlords of the humans were provided with the **contact functions** of the **Second** stone in order to communicate directly with the Anunnaki. The pieces together are regarded as one segment, along with the **staff or the key of Aaron** which is the instrument to activate the systems. It is far easier to keep these items together on earth as they were in easy reach for the early settlers to keep control and follow the whereabouts of the gems.

This earthly key is only an Anunnaki communicator as far as the humans were concerned amongst other functions. The generator or signal beacon within the Star Stone was handed over to the Levite monks along with the hybrid Igigi protector within the colony. And we knew that if all the keys were to be given to mankind which are known as the (Nergal Construct) in their entirety

'The Seed': 'Anu – Nexus'

then the human leaders would have simply destroyed their own existence should they ever have managed to understand their true destructive powers.

But where modern man has gained the knowledge of nuclear fusion and fission is a question that the **rogue Claw** and other universal outcast species will have to face trial by the council of five to account for their mis-use of such knowledge, which was most likely given to the earth scientists.

But let me inform you that each planet within the **nine gates** do possess such segments of the Star Stone located on their home planets. Nine planets and nine segments. Each tablet is connected to each other like a communications network in its make-up and sits in direct harmony with the other segments and emits large energy pulses that constantly communicate and update their unique positions in each star constellation within the known universe exactly the same way as mankind tracks their nuclear weapons on earth. I should also add that each Star Stone is also assigned a protective 'guardian' And a person that travels through time as the **Star Stone protector**. The Igigi normally have this duty on earth, but, I see you also carry the bracelet of the ancient 'Anunnaki' on your wrist. This is your guardian protective amulet against being destroyed by the very destructive powers of the Nergal relic. That is of course should you ever encounter the relic or be exposed to it physically. You may be the human Protector of this icon today and just do not know it yet. Most likely your arm clasp was once worn by a great Anunnaki protector or Levite cleric priest of the ancient days no doubt. We as Merlithian are not protected in this way by this mighty ancient power and most likely that is why Lilith has devised a plan where you and the human hybrids should join with An'Mer and the team in support to slaughter and eradicate the rogue Draco claw clan. You must be very aware that the Claw are a horrible deadly unhinged toxic breed, and they hold no regard for life whatsoever and will likely attempt to steal the 'Earth Ark' Star Stone tablets if they can get the chance. And then use the technology and the destructive powers to activate another nuclear attack on either this planet or another and that is why Lilith is worried that it may be Mars.

Hence why, we have been summoned here to Antarctica.' Hastings pondered on her responses for a while before retorting. 'An 'Laara is this why? the Pleiadian talk of the triad great awakening along with this covenant thing. What does this mean for humanity?' An 'Laara pondered on his questions for a while longer then swept her long red leather robe to one side as her eyes suddenly lit up in a firey green haze, as she spoke. 'The great kings of the ancient Northern realm as an example are entities what we the Anunnaki call the last remaining over lords of the underworld and the **First** of these powerful deities is the **Valkyrie Queen,** who is a dangerous wonder of the

Norske and Hades underworld environments. She is the torch bearer and eternal guide of the Norse departed souls and commands the dead who were taken by the angry battle sword during the great Icelandic uprisings. These soldiers of misfortune are known as the undead army and remain at her call and command in the afterlife, a realm that humans may not experience. Although, An'Freya dwells mostly in the mists of the **Folkvangr** lands and very rarely leaves that plain of existence. But, on the other side of Nordic demise the great and the good dwell in a place called **Valhalla** and remain there in the afterlife in a closed gateway or a 5th dimension and can never return to earth in the physical form. The great entities you know as ancient Gods, Kings or Queens cannot penetrate beyond their plains of existence. And by decree they can never inhabit the same time dimension more than once in their whole evolution span. Hence, why the Pleiadian vibrational **'Sphere'** was created, this is a very special place in time where the overlords can tap into a frequency and communicate spiritually with one another. But there can never be any overlap of plains as they can send ripples of disruption through the balance of time. As an example, the Nordic Queen **An 'Freya'** is the exception to the rule, as an ancient wise female and Anunnaki hybrid she roams the netherworld and flirts within the time and space realm as once did Lilith.

But she can both penetrate the physical and metaphysical therefore, she can manifest herself in a solid state and deal with rogue 'fallen angels' who have physically crossed plains, but this is very uncommon. She is the balance of the Nordic realms and the nexus between human dominion and northern myth cultures. Her existence on earth is signified by the presence of two great **Harpy Eagles** or raptors which are wonderous but deadly birds of prey. The avian has slate feathers and their underside is mostly white plumage apart from the 'tarsi' or the back which is striped with black feathers. The beast sits at over four foot in height sitting on its incredibly large and strong deadly talons. The eyes of this wonderous bird are embedded with grey irises, but in the Viking Harpy species these are deep red. The animal weighs in at between fifteen to twenty pounds and can knock a man over with one swift swipe of its powerful raptor wings which can spread to almost four feet if not more in length. The Harpy are a danger even to the Anunnaki. And, our Anunnaki Folklore has this bird depicted as the living spirits of the Viking dead and they travel wherever An'Freya decides to dwell. A warning for you, if you spy this raptor or be in its presence at any time you must take great care and avoid close contact at all costs.

'The Seed': 'Anu – Nexus'

The second power of the Triad of Kings is the Ionian King - Koenig '**An Tura**' who is another great Alban warlord of the Northern Islands and he is armed with the Tartarus inferni sword of 'Ex Kal' – (the ancient sword of enlightenment), a weapon that only serves to eradicate tyranny and injustice for the people for which it serves, this King is the most feared across all the Anunnaki folklore, as An 'Tura' serves the righteous and commands the middle heavens. We or should I say the Anunnaki Pantheon whilst in the **vibrational plain** will always yield to his power and grace.

The third gracious royal seed you know as Kilkamesh (Gilgames') or the Anunnaki King. And together they form the eternal power of the Anunnaki Nexus'. These great lords who protect the balance of the heavens using the Keys of Nergal as controlling instruments which as I have alluded to earlier. The star stone gems collectively are the energy sources that harmonise the Nergal construct. The Keys of which Earth, Orion and Mars are bound by the **Anunnaki covenant**, and a further explanation to answer your earlier question.

One key was once located under the Great Sphinx control complex at Giza but that may have been moved to Ethiopia, the **Second key** is located in the country known as Scotland and is located on an island called Iona and the **Third key** is on the planet Almintak in the Orion cluster. As far as Earth is concerned the Earthly Keys of Nergal were originally placed with the Mesopotamians and watched over by the Igigi people for many centuries. If one was to be successful in bringing any of the nine keys together or at least three, then that entity could potentially render the holocaust weapons inert, thus removing any potential outcome of nuclear war, or conversely, could activate the weapons and destroy what we know as the universe.'

Hastings then very nonchalantly cast a glance over at the plinths that sat in the corner of the Habitat hibernation chamber then back at An'Laara. 'So, if we are to eradicate the Draco Claw clan given that they the Draco could execute a nuclear strike. Surely, we are bound by the covenant to disturb our great lords as those who are in stasis here in Antarctica and bring the Triad together?' Or do we evoke the ethereal Enlil, Enki, Ninhursag, Nanna Utu or Inanna to bring all the Anunnaki dominion into existence and employ their great knowledge of the ancient serpent people.' An 'Laara, took a step closer towards Hastings and then tilted her head to one side again. 'You are well informed about our Aunnaki lineage. The Triad would probably think that this would be below their status level for such an intervention and would see this uprising by the Claw as a minor inconvenience to deal with, especially for such an endeavour as taking on a single clutch of lizards and cause their '**awakening**' which, I think would be deemed an inconvenience to them.

And besides Lilith is awake and she has already determined the strategy of closing down the Draco, however, if we do suffer any defeat by the Claw then the Triad would certainly intervene at some point and that I am sure of. Lilith will have already considered this option, as she is more than capable of dealing with the Draco if we stand together and execute her plan. And furthermore, we cannot call on the ancient Anunnaki at this time as they are gathered on the planet Mintaka in the Orion cluster for King Alalu's departure festival and will not leave until the problems of the 'third planet' are solved.

The Triad have only been summoned once in my knowledge and that was when the heavens had fallen into chaos more than eight thousand earth years ago. The aftermath of their involvement was catastrophic and nearly destroyed the Orion cluster in its entirety. However, it was that single event that harmonised what you see as the collaboration of interplanetary co-operation today. Anyway, back to the Merlithian people, and what you do not know is that we are pure Anunnaki and can deal with the Draco, albeit, Lilith has decreed that yourself and the hybrids join An'Mer in this war and remove the Draco along with their DNA seed from our planets. Having said all that, there is another problem much closer to the human home you need to understand as well, and this is the most problematic of all. The world leaders you know as Kings and Queens and political leaders appear to have very similar blood groups and this will be their downfall as they have evolved as an unhinged inbred secret human society. And the Anunnaki may decide to release a toxic blood antagen and remove them from their existence once and for all. This action has dire consequences however, the fallout may lead to the decline of many countries. The alternative option is for the Anunnaki is to reinstall **new emperors** to oversee mankind until they can be trusted with their own destiny, and that will setback the Anunnaki matrix construct considerably.' An' Laara then stood up and thanked Hastings for his precious time and left the chamber.

Chapter Seventeen:

'Antigen'

An' Chilles & An'Nanu

The Anunnaki bioscientists An' Chilles and An'Nanu were working in the laboratory when An'Chilles had identified the specific enzyme that targets a designated blood group and through process she had already engineered the enzymes that can potentially **destroy** humans that fall within the realms of **'The Purple Royal Bloodline'. (Rhesus Negative - The blood of the monkey**) and blood of the ancients (haplogroup R1b1a2).The target people were to be two generations stemming back in time across global sectors, and then a systematic DNA removal from thereon would begin. The Anunnaki knew and understood only too well that some innocent people may die as a result of this action. But it was going to be far easier to control this action than having yet another great deluge or another nuclear strike to recover from. Albeit, if the current monarchies of the world were to survive into the next century, then it was only a matter of time before the **'End of Days'** would be unleashed on the human population of the planet through more uncontrolled inbreeding, and their guaranteed use of potentially ultra-destructive nuclear weapons was a given. Especially if they evolve enough to understand the systems in their entirety, thus destroying the Anunnaki master construct. An'Chilles had tagged the carbohydrate chains and diluted the amino acids with some other substance and then grouped them together within the glob of blood depleting enzymes which would in essence simply break down the **liver** of the host and bring their human existence to a rapid end or at least that was the theory as An'Chilles hoped. She surmised that the opposing blood cells of both Positive and Negative would interact and reject one another on contact and the lineage would therefore cease to prorecreate. Modern scientists would call this the blood **inhibition test** on the basis where agglutination fails to occur and the host simply dies of acute organ failure mainly in the liver but does indeed affect other organs. However, if the real numbers of people within the Royal bloodline were counted today it would stem into perhaps millions from over the centuries, hence, this is the why?

the segmented approach would keep a reasonable amount of people safe from extinction whilst targeting only the recent royal offspring, then again, the real issue is the unknown amount of unrecorded bastard Royal babies that were born across the globe. But, nevertheless mankind's politicians and their monarchy must be reminded of their place in the grander scheme of life and not all will see or lead a happy and fruitful life especially, those individuals that sanctioned the raising of the Anunnaki from their hibernation hives. This vengeful action is a subtle revenge tactic to ensure that the Anunnaki surgically remove all those world leaders who had made conscious decisions to try and rule mankind, but humans have forgotten that the **Anunnaki Covenant** which is many hundreds of centuries old, is absolute and the Anunnaki have dealt with humans in this way for quite some time.

An' Chilles raised up the small medical clay phial in front of her eyes and chinked the beaker with her forefinger, she then gazed into the blue liquid in the acorn shaped receptacle as it turned from a clear solution into a red solution for a few seconds and then turned into a purple pulp, then finally into a pinkish pigmented ooze. She then handed the phial over to An'Nanu for testing. 'It looks like this is the right formula we need, can you please test it and see if we have got the recipe correct?'

An'Nanu gazed over the clay pot and was very amused for quite sometime then responded. 'An'Chilles this concoction is highly dangerous and can wipe out the Anunnaki as well. We must ensure one hundred percent that we never come into contact with this potion ever again, then placed the clay pot into a glass bottle and sealed the lid. We must also warn the Merlithian what this really is. The humans must be tested also to ensure that they are not of any royal bloodline, I mean Hastings himself may well be a strong contender to fall foul of this killer potion.'

An'Chilles then drew her hand across her face then commented further. 'The Anunnaki original bloodline is strong enough to fight off this mild mix, but I do agree that the three humans must also be tested and we should also cover the Merlithian, we would be deemed very neglectful if we did not protect our own first.' An'Chilles and An'Nanu smiled at one another then continued with their special laboratory duties. Their job was done and the Anunnaki **mutant enzyme** was prepared for the end of humankind's royal lineage and perhaps several political world leaders.

An 'Chilles then wrote a small note in her records:- **for HK/Enz/Blood Dilution/ Rh Positive/anti Negative diluted expiry /2027/06.**

Chapter Eighteen:

'Sitchin's Flying Machines'

The origins of the Draco (Snake) species have always been obscured in complex historical detail along with their true journey of an alien creation and once sat within the Anunnaki hierarchy. The Pleiadian book of records should state that the Deep Space Dragons had once been a rogue set of colonial intergalactic 'Claw' criminals who had escaped dominion capture and had started another colonial life somewhere deep in the Andromeda belt. The definition of Claw as a matter on context was an Anunnaki term signifying an unclassed species.

(latin translation) - **CLAW**- *Crede Ligitimus Annulled Warrior.*

As a result of their expulsion the Claw had subsequently ventured farther afield from the Andromeda belt and found the planet earth and had rapidly adopted the heavenly body as a new power domain. However, as far as humans are concerned Greek mythology seems to have picked up on the toxic Dragon myths and legends in more comprehensive coverage than other subject matter concerning the gods. Especially as one of their great giants fought with the early Olympians and battled for ten years as multiple deaths ensued until the great 'Athena' despatched the entity back into the skies with its dragon tail tucked firmly within its hind quarters and eventually formed the 'Starry' North celestial Pole. In Dragon Draco myths the **'Apple'** is once again classed as the seed or fruit of life and we see another overlap of legends of the great gardens and further reference to apples paving the way for a new legacy. Hitherto, we can touch on the Golden apples of the **Hesperides** as another fine recorded example which involved a group of mischievous nymphs and elves who were said to be the real guardians of the tree of life. Who with the assistance and aid of a watchful dragon protected the gateway to the Northern stars. These Guardians watched over the tree of golden apples in a garden located beyond the Atlas Mountains at the western border of a place known as Oceanus. Perhaps back then this was the eternally flowing river of the **Euphrates** or the **Tigris** encircling their known world of dominion life. Which was thought to capture the complete internal world at that time, or conversely, the location could be mythical and taken literally as the heavenly river Styx in the stars.

Another ancient legend depicts the great labours of **Hercules** who stole the golden apple and killed Ladon and was subsequently formed into another star constellation by the greater gods. With all these fables and legends, it should be noted that when discussing Anunnaki as subject matter we may have to ensure that mankind understands or at least acknowledges that the Draco were once a significant breed within the alien mix as this part of creation as a recognised Draco serpent icon. And we can find that the great Hercules depicted and carved on many glyths and stones appearing to stomp on the head of the Draco king in his desire for all the gods to witness his ultimate power. Thus, he was as an entity demonstrating his drive, wrath and desire for ruling the humankind domain. This depiction can be taken as very much symbolic of the **Anunnaki** in their endeavours of laying down the seeds of law within the cosmos, and not too long thereafter. The unprecedented uprising on Mars may have occurred, albeit, up until that point was when the Draco relationships was quite peaceful between them and the Anunnaki.

But common interest and relationships between the two species today have since turned very sour and deadly. At this juncture regarding our ongoing education, we can turn to the ancient Babylonians who succeeded the Sumerian people and therefore, should understand that the creation of Trigonometry, Science, Art, Music, Geology Mathematics and Agriculture along with things we take for granted today as examples of learning and formed parts of many theories, but 'Trig' was first established around one thousand years before the Greeks had started recording the movement of the heavenly bodies. This is an important fact because chiefly it provides an ancient chronological timeline and milestone to refer to where man had started to think and stood out as a stand-alone being with their own ideas and notions. Hence why rationale thinking points to the arrival of the **Anunnaki star people** on earth, and their interventions should in hypothesis be given a fair credit score.

There is no great argument that the Sumerian culture had laid down the very early seeds of civilisation and watched humanity grow and eventually flourish. The question we should be asking is? 'Did the Sumerian ancient culture really gain assistance from these star people?' And that they may have been exposed to ancient out of world technologies such as advanced mathematics and life sciences. However, if this is not the case then we must also ask? If not! Then! who did? In the annals of the Anunnaki construct this is undisputable fact that these heavenly visitors had indeed intervened and raised their hybrid children as new intellectuals and we can turn to the Sumerian Cunieform tablet script records that do highlight that the Sumer people maintained their highly informative detailed records from thousands of years prior, and captured very intricate detail of their daily lives and to this end a note is referenced to the terminology used to describe the term **'Flying Machines'** where Zecharia Sitchin the Azerbaijani scientist who could be deemed the better or more informed authority on the Sumerian language in most cases at this time, and he had certainly thought this terminology referred to alien flying craft. However, we must remain mindful on the subject matter of which Zecharia and some of his important assumptions were made, and could have been lost in his early translations, or he may have added his own fanciful perspective on life off this planet views, but nevertheless this record should never be dismissed. Of course, the Greeks and Roman scholars identified these aircraft as **'flying shields'** and is highly suggestive to the shape of a flying saucer.

Chapter Nineteen:

'Dendera'

As the Pleiadian craft landed at the Dendera Temple complex which is located about two and half kilometres south-east of Dendera, Hathor (Abydos) Egypt. Hastings and his colleagues had exited the small craft and had made their way to the main temple entrance. Having just walked through the great hallway between the twenty-four highly decorated great columns that dominated the inner space, they reached the range of recesses and vaults where Hastings could feel the immediate sensation of what he could only describe as acute electrical vibrations in the atmosphere. These were pulses that were rippling up through his spine. He then gazed upon the many wall panels and colourful inscriptions then remarked to his colleagues that this was indeed a place that was significant in the game of astral connections. 'Wow! He cried out slowly! 'This is awesome, look at this place, I have never experienced this feeling of peacefulness before. Erica, can you feel that rhythm in the air, this, is just simply amazing, I think there is a deep soul presence in this temple and it is soft and yet so powerful, I am sure that the Pleiadian have chosen this house of gateways for very good reason.' Erica and Darlene had become unusually quiet and were clearly subdued by their surroundings and were sauntering around the shrine and stroking each of the columns in turn whilst taking time to view the intense imagery as the huge structures reached up to the very apex of the building. It was abundantly clear that the columns supported a roof structure that was certainly a lot older in construction by many centuries before the Greeks had rebuilt the complex back in antiquity.

Hastings glanced around the temple and then back at the girls and was momentarily taken back and quite amused as they both appeared to be in a state of casual flux or were simply lost in their own minds as he had observed that both Darlene and Erica's' eyes had a striking blue tint of light around them, it was as if their aura's had been awakened, even more so as they danced around appearing to be very relaxed in their overall demeanour. Darlene was first to comment. 'I think I really belong here, I mean look at this colour and design, it is out of this world Kemp, but, I had no idea that this house of Horus even existed, I wonder why our guides at Ahgartha had never mentioned this temple before. I mean it is so peaceful that I could literally die in here.'

Erica was also in a nonchalant state of mind and was now walking slowly in between every column becoming emotionally excited then remarked. 'Kemp, my hands and fingers are tingling, I can feel every movement of these glyphs, I can feel the floor pulsing up through my toes.' Hastings halted for a moment and waited patiently for the girls to get closer before they ascended the unusually uneven and flattened stairway then entered what he thought was an anti-chamber. After a few moments of being quite literally stunned and mesmerised by the sight before him, he then gazed upwards at the ceiling, only to find the great **Dendera zodiac** of the Pleiadian solar system was towering over him like a huge circular star map depicting the thirty-six god like effigies that had been etched and painted into the concentric edge of the plan. Each entity appearing to cover or had been assigned ten days of the annual calendar cycle, embellished with the very recognisable twelve-star constellations that even he could make out. He slowly shook his head in wonder.

'There you go girls twelve stars, and many recognisable figures, and look up there, I wonder if this is the **'roadmap'** to our human creation or even our origins. I honestly feel this is where I think the Anunnaki had kept the **seven Hathor maidens** of creation hidden.

And used this place as an Anunnaki breeding maternity hospital.' Darlene on hearing his words was almost tearful as she spoke very softly having been struck by the deep strong emotion and the overall atmosphere of their surroundings. 'You have no idea what you have just said Kemp, this is certainly a place of deep relaxation and if I was ever to state that a building was feminine in its construction, then this temple is obviously it. Certainly not a tomb, but, a great place of worship. Well not for all our earthbound species anyway, but this place is the house of the eternal life and happiness. Can you not feel that divine presence rippling and pulsing up through your veins? Look, if there are twelve planetary constellations then we must have twelve-star colonies, that must mean that the race of people who inhabited here knew and understood that this must have been a **'time portal'** of some kind and maybe it is still highly active.' Erica then stepped forward.

'Over there, look! I see that the great bear star cluster is the most prominent, and over there Darlene, the sign of Cancer. I think the Pleiadies constellation appears to be very central if you look hard enough.' Hastings took a very deep breath and then grabbed the hands of both the girls.

'Ladies, let us not get too hung up yet on this place, we have all been through a hell of a lot of experiences over the last few years and we have witnessed things that mortal man would never understand. Remember there is something happening in the cosmos between some powerful and ancient 'Out of this world' species that are most likely going to war. And, if this place has been chosen to start this campaign, then, I am sure the Anunnaki know exactly what they are doing.' As Hastings and the girls stepped out from the star-chamber they realised that they were not alone. Other visitors were already present. Three figures actually. One figure presented himself as the Igigi chief consort on earth known as '**Talus Anu** or TA' for short. The consort TA was indeed human in his physical make up and stood at five foot eight and was clad in traditional Egyptian robes and carried two lotus leaves in his hands. He then extended a welcome handshake to Kemp Hastings who, was somewhat taken by surprise to find that '**TA**' knew not only of his physical existence but also why he had travelled to Hathor with the team on his secret mission. 'Welcome to the Hathor powerhouse ladies and yourself mister Hastings. These people here are from the Igigi species, they are my helpers. We have been waiting for you and your colleagues to arrive for quite some time.' He then presented a single golden lotus leaf to each of the girls. 'For you, my Princesses, and it is with the greatest of pleasures to be introduced to three different species at one time, most delightful, although, I also should say that I do not envy your mammoth task ahead of you. Especially as to deal with this clutch of Draco insurgents, nasty breed, nasty business. As they are a formidable and very toxic species to deal with in general. You will need all the help you can muster for this campaign. We understand that the Draco Claw have recently sent several long-range scout drones to San Katerina in both Sinai and the Tripex at Giza, and that means an unregistered craft must be here on our planet. So may I suggest that you all lay low here for a while until we can destroy these eyes in the sky. The Draco are not exactly as highly versatile nor as mobile as we are, but we do anticipate that they will not wait long before more of their clan arrive at the American base or perhaps, they are already on site. And to be honest we really do not possess the resources we require as yet to war directly with them. Although, I understand that the Merlithian breed have also been activated, and that was indeed a new fantastic revelation to unfold and should provide us a reasonable amount of powerful force in order to face Shamgaz.

By all accounts the 'Claw' have taken over the complete DARPA establishment and are accelerating their own hybrid colony, or resurrecting the old ones. And this drive must be thwarted soonest. Once the Claw have amassed in their numbers, they will most likely become unstoppable.'

Hastings then gazed over the Dendera temple and responded. 'So, this is the great Hathor? the temple of illumination, the House of Horus?' He asked quizzingly. TA waited for a moment or two before answering. 'Yes! it is, and how very perceptive of you, it was once the old test bed for Anunnaki development of energy vibration and used for the production of the gold-based manna bread, and of course the lighting clusters for illuminating the deeper sub terranean chambers, designed for all their or should I say our locations. But in fact, was mostly designed for underground smelting work. The structure itself was constructed as a deep energy vibration silo and conversion facility. So, please be careful where you place your hands within these cells. Many parts are still radio-active, but you will be quite safe, because as far as I am aware it is mostly **inert** in key places that we are going to be located. Apart from the phoenix zeta building out in the courtyard. The project was quite successful back then. But over time the **powerhouse** was moved to another location in Lebanon at (Baalbek) where the heavy cargo craft dropped off supplies. For your enlightenment folks there also exists another manna works house dedicated to the Hathor in the mountain tops of mount **Herob** in the Saudi peninsula. People tend to forget that Egypt and Saudi Arabia once formed a great single nation. The 'Herob' is known to the Anunnaki as the manna smelting, production and storage facility where vast amounts physical gold was transformed or transmuted into the lighter than light bread of the gods and classed as monoatomic white gold. Once transformed the **manna** was then shipped into the heavens.

Perhaps. I should also mention that this fine powder in this ultra-fine state was also physically consumed by the Anunnaki and several Pharaohs who, could transcend back and forth into the ethereal heavens at their leisure. This golden dust has super hallucinogenic powers and healing qualities that I do not really understand, but the mount of Horeb facility was an industrial complex on a large scale that today has been shrouded in great mystery and is protected by the laws of the land for good reason. I understand that in the last century the discovery of the laboratories revealed a great tonnage of manna gold powder about fifty metric tons that was secretly removed and perhaps we will never know its true whereabouts today as the explorers had taken great efforts to hide it.

Maybe one could **dig up** the explorers Flinders Petrie and ask him. As exactly what he had done to the ancients. We could also align the Giza plant as well as a similar but smaller facility where the super-heated internal production laboratories in the Kings and Queen chambers were closer to home for the deities, and their conical bread 'Bakers' the metallurgists who baked the bread of heaven as required. Dendera however is a complex build for the Anunnaki and most likely the last facility before they moved operations to Ahgartha in Antarctica. Well, that was about two and half to three thousand earth years ago of course. Then the Greek people arrived at Hathor, and what an amazing job they did of rebuilding this temple as it should be. But even today the structure looks fairly well preserved considering it was just a factory of sorts mainly due to its strategic location over the magnetic telluric energy bed. And Abydos was still far enough away to be hidden from the Claw and other troublemakers. Although the Anunnaki may have used the particle accelerators to upgrade their beacons at Tripex at Giza recently. And we also think that the Pleiadians can still activate what they call the zeta gateways from here in the same manner as the Anunnaki do for Katerina but, it has been a very long time since this domain has been reset.

Although, we must be careful as we feel that our electronic signature can become an issue especially if the Draco are monitoring telluric ley line activity and identify our location. But. we think that this works in our favour because monitoring over forty thousand and fifty-seven kilometres of magnetic fairways won't be an easy task for them to achieve. Remember folks Hathor also sits on a huge magnetic energy field that was once deemed the central hub of the universe, or so I am told, I really don't know, as we are only provided a certain amount of information regarding the real workings of the cosmos.

Probably better that way. Anyway, back to the project here at Hathor. This temple became a fairly important place in real terms as the Anunnaki had simultaneously devised a more convenient way of illuminating the granite stonework by introducing ion particle dust that sparkled when exposed to magnetism and became quite a novelty. Prior to that a great many of oiled lamps filled the many non-essential spaces and of course were removed. But, sadly this new breakthrough was very short lived and the complex was eventually completed. And, I must admit though, this condition saved a lot of effort in constructing a new and very cumbersome and vulnerable lighting system out of clay jars as was the Babylon batteries. Although the energy within the smelting works was intense and of course the vibration plain covered many plains or dimensions across the universe and could be penetrated from here.

Today, the temple does serve a modern-day purpose. And it is a very good distraction for keeping the thousands of visitors amused. We should not be disturbed in this place for now at least. Please be careful though when you enter the lower chambers as there will be residual static energy present especially around the **'Necklace'** chambers and of course what the modern

'The Seed': 'Anu – Nexus'

people will call the '**Lower Crypt area**', but it is not really a crypt it is actually a part of the zeta vortex shell.

We know that at some point during the alchemic operations that most of the stairwells were physically melted by a lashing of super-heated titan mercury and sulphur as the ancient scientists produced their important manna and had experimented with many chemicals from the alchemic tables, when there was an uncontrolled release from the containment shell quite literally exploded and softened the stone floor slabs and parts of the lower walls. Thank goodness it was a low volume release as the whole lower chambers could have been destroyed completely. So please be careful as you negotiate the stair treads as they are very uneven, and if you want to understand the extreme power of what titan mercury under extreme pressure and heat can achieve. Then just take a look as to how the ancient city of Tanis suffered when an underground titan chamber exploded and sent a catastrophic wave of plasma and mercury paste over the entire complex, which pretty much levelled the place. However, you should not believe all the fabled myths and legends about when the 'Greek Fire' machine that was used against the early population in the battle of the second Thebes war. Just more modern day cover up mis-direction and utter poppycock. Especially when the huge arms were blown off tall solid twenty to thirty-ton granite statues and obelisks that were struck along with the thick heavy granite walls of buildings that had simply melted.

You just have to think back to Sodom and Ghomorra as a quick reminder. Same destruction, same power source just a different method of delivery.' Hastings suddenly sparked up thinking that what he thought he knew about Egyptian history and this manna gold stuff, but then reminded himself that he was obviously ignorant to the real truth of the ancients, then reacted.

'Well, there you go folks, every day, is a learning day as they say.' He muttered as TA smiled back at him and continued with his deep knowledge of the Peiadian sanctuary. 'And I must say that through the efforts of Ptolemy in his defence he managed to lay the seeds of long-term development with his successors even with uneven stairs. You will find ladies and yourself mister Kemp that the real schematics of this place can still be found on the many glyphs scattered across the inner walls. Although, they are a wee bit out of date, but in reality, still great testament to Anunnaki endurance and astral navigation. Osiris himself almost perfected this project but succeeded by all accounts in the absence of his Anunnaki handler. And, I have just remembered. There were also two other low level titan mercury releases or underground events at both Giza and at Sakkara in antiquity. A few very important lessons learned before the Anunnaki had perfected the process of course, the idea of mixing sulphur, mercury and titan steel gloop together. What a mistake that was. But, with hindsight this place Hathor eventually found the true energy balance and was still quite an accomplishment for such a junior entity to achieve.

Anyway, folks all that aside we have been tasked to setup a command cell inside what the clerics call the '**Birthing chamber**', you will of course recognise the sacred birthing pool that pretty much mirrors the grand chamber under the Sphinx complex as they are similar in build and design. The birthing pool here is dry presently but be aware it can re-energise and refill quite rapidly especially when we start to power up the titan vibration generator for the Pleiadian people.

This will keep us quite cool as the system sends fresh air that will circumvent within the structure. And, because of your body sizes as well it will also be much easier for you to enter and negotiate the lower crypt area as you may have to crouch down a little and may have to endure some discomfort whilst descending and ascending in some very tight spaces. And as you know the Anunnaki spinal seven stage 'shakra' column cannot be subject to any acute or excessive physical twisting or bending, hence, why it was a good idea to bring you folks along.

More so, for getting into really small and tight spaces where the Draco cannot enter. Please also understand that this part of the cosmic conundrum regarding this temple is that this beautiful place was once inhabited by seven space maidens from the Pleiadies constellation and they in turn ventured far across the globe to set in place the framework for learning and development whilst nurturing the new Anunnaki species in their designated countries. There are many Hathor Temples folks, and seven distinct ones, and I should add that Hathor is the primary temple, and it will function when the time is right and will be illuminated with this ancient technology. But only for a short time. There is also the manna Temple in Saudi that is also dedicated to Hathor as I had said earlier. Every now and again we do witness ultra-violet and strange neon lights appearing on occasions as the temple changes its vibrational footprint and alters the time axis when different star alignments take place, and we have witnessed one recently when the planet Nibiru crossed the path of the 'Nexus' Nebula like heavenly souls passing in the night sky as they re-energise.'

Hastings then responded. 'Ah yes, flashing lights, souls in the night sky, heavenly maidens, that reminds me that the girls need to re-energise themselves after their long journey of nearly two hours in those '**Go globes**' and I certainly will not complain myself about the Pleiadean craft either. Very efficient but not too comfortable for the human physical form, I should say.'

TA then smiled. 'Yes, but a necessary evil, you must understand that, if the Draco get wind that humans are involved in this assault, they will simply start murdering all people on sight as they are deemed a certain inconvenience as a species. Or the Claw will have already micro chipped a few key people in order to create the **illusion** that all is normal at the centre. Any human or soldier you encounter in DARPA will have already been potentially mind probed or even micro-chipped. So please just remember they are simulant **'drones'** and you might be talking directly with the Draco face to face and never really know it. But the human element or responsive presence will remain cold and inert with no signs of real human emotions, I am sure only humans can read these signs.

You could use this to your advantage. The Claw have also reduced the American laboratory crew and only a few scientists may still remain. They have quite literally sealed off the complete perimeter of the camp. The scientists you meet will not be normal humans either and they will be under the Draco influence as are the soldiery having been fitted with **mind-inserts** for direct control. Hence why this **DARPA facility** was researching mind probes in the earlier days. It works like a remote control for a human but activated at very low-level vibrational frequencies via an insert within the human brain. And I must admit some of the human minds are more advanced than we gave them credit for, as we understand their advancement but that's the military mindset for you.'

Hastings then turned to the girls and asked them a very direct question? 'Are you two beings snake drones or are you real fully blooded, self-thinking highly emotional intellectual and beautiful females of the species they call the human?' He then raised his hands in the air and started to wave at them very spookily and practically scared the girls as they each stepped backwards whilst grabbing at their hand satchels.

Darlene was first to respond to his childish outburst and his actions. 'Kemp what the name in Hades are you doing? have you been sniffing the **'titan gloop'** again or have you been at those arctic magic mushrooms.' Hastings had almost composed himself and was smiling back at the girls in a very childish manner. 'Ladies c'mon this is the temple of Hathor, the house of Horus, the temple of peace and universal tranquillity and of course, the ancient house of gross sexual debauchery and lust. The gods have also dwelled here and Osiris and Cleopatra themselves have even dominated this beautiful place, and look we are their guests. What do you think of that so far ladies? we are in the most ancient **'knocking shop'** and monoatomic **'drug centre'** in history of mankind or at least one of them!'

Erica flicked her hair to one side and commented. 'You really need to get some serious medical therapy and professional help you know, even the Anunnaki have excellent medical practitioners, and they can give you a frontal lobotomy or something similar to get your male urges seen to.' Meanwhile, as Hastings stood rubbing his eyes in pretence of crying he put on a very false sad face. The girls were laughing as opposed to earlier having been immersed in an emotional state of flux. **TA,** on the other hand was watching in total amazement as most likely he had never been exposed to the human sense of humour before. And as he shook his head to and fro he became aware that a smooth scirocco of warm wind had swept silently by them and swirled for a few minutes within the array of the huge columns in the inner sanctum of the temple.

Then Erica spoke straight out of the blue very softly in her current state of mind. 'The **elementals** are here, and I don't mean minor ones either. These are the ancient powerful and experienced. I can feel their linear vibrations in this place, can you feel that too Darlene.' Hastings placed his right hand on her shoulder and spoke. 'Looks like we now know why you girls are here after all then Erica. You see TA, the Arcturians and the Pleidians have this unique ability to sense emotion, danger and peace within these chamber halls. Perhaps they both have returned to this place from an earlier existence to repeat more happier time in their lives.'

Darlene had also eased herself forward and reached out and had touched Erica's other shoulder then she also spoke. 'I can feel it too, it is very strong. There is a great sense of peace and definite serenity here, but there is also a strong potent presence. It is a divine entity or maybe it could be that of Hathor herself. And if she is not here physically! Then she is certainly watching us spiritually.' TA then clapped his hands together and the trio suddenly broke their concentration and slowly stepped away from one another as TA interjected. 'If, I can continue folks. We still have work to do! You may also need to find an appropriate disguise, perhaps a military style uniform to penetrate DARPA, and possibly move around unnoticed within the base. I think that would be more accommodating and you may be easily dismissed as common soldiery when you get into the camp area. You would have to mimic the soldiers in their mode of moving and speaking within the complex of course. The Draco will certainly not expect that in any such case. I am sure the Merlithian team will be here shortly, as I cannot wait to meet them, I understand that they have gone to San Katerina to pick up some instruments. Hopefully, they have been and gone before the Draco drones spy them.

Listen folks, the Draco Claw will know that we are doing something in response to their efforts, but they will never anticipate or suspect in a million years of ever being confronted by humans directly. I would suggest you also use this element of surprise to your advantage. Although, we do understand that the world outside DARPA runs as normal or at least that's what the Draco want the external human world to think. But there may be an option in how we can enter the complex without detection. We know that the supplies and food restock convoy is specially designed for delivering aquatic food sources to the station and will be going to drop the replenishment off tomorrow evening.' TA and Hastings had then moved away from the earshot of the girls who were now caressing the large columns in the temple again and sort of chasing the elemental winds.

TA almost placed his hand on the staff of the Ankh as he talked. And Hastings swiftly responded. 'I do not think you really want to do that! This thing does some weird shit and wonderful things as it carries a power source that I do not yet understand, but I would suggest you best stay clear of it, or you may actually sustain a real **'bite'** from this rod as history as shown us regarding staffs and rods of the ancients, Aaron's being particularly powerful. But, please carry on. You mentioned the truck of fish.'

TA then pulled his arms back rapidly and thought about wanting to impulsively just reach out and grab the staff of the great **Ankh** and hold it just for a few seconds. And this would have been enough to quench his desire for experiencing the hidden power of the ancients. But he knew instinctively that Hasting's was not joking when he spoke about hidden powers and any ancient snake relics or their hidden powers and continued to engage with his master plan.

'Well, this replenishment is delivered as fresh fish that are contained within large holding tanks of seawater, if we can find a way to immerse your team into the holding tank then you could gain entrance into DARPA, duly escape from the tanks and then open the gates.' Hastings shook his head from side to side in shock and almost amazement let alone disbelief whilst holding back a very desperate grin in an attempt not to laugh out too loudly nor embarrass TA. And then posed a question. 'TA, what sort of aquatic life are we talking about here in these tanks?' TA then rubbed his little fat chin and pondered on the answer and took a wild guess as Hastings contemplated the TA grand master plan. Whilst thinking about how ludicrous the concept actually sounded in theory let alone in real practicality.

Then the reply came. 'Dolphins and zooplankton and a large amount of king shrimpy things, I think. The trucks are parked up overnight at the eastern end of the complex, and then, in the morning they are drained through a large suction delivery umbilical tube into the main complex. All we have to do is break free from the tank once inside the complex.' Hastings was smirking again but even more so and responded with a few flippant remarks. 'So, let me get this correct, you want us to hide in a giant fish tank with dolphins and creepy zooplankton sea creatures, then just break free. After which we attack the Claw. Is that what you call your strategic thinking? But, there is one little miniscule detail I need to know. Tell me how on earth will we all be able to breathe whilst we are in transit?' TA then smiled a huge broad grin.

'We have high technical underwater breathing apparatus, the breathing gear is no larger than the size of your hand, it's a mesh membrane just like a soft facemask that is pulled over your face which will keep you alive for years if need be. It is like oxygen from the trees that go into your lungs but this mesh removes the salts from the water and replaces the salts with treated oxygen through an attachment, it is just an older Venusian underwater-mining piece of breathing gear.' Hastings was shaking his head again in disbelief then made another statement.

'And we will all be in the same tank together with these aquatic creatures? Pardon me TA for being just a little bit sceptical here, but this plan? we could all potentially become fish sushi quite rapidly, I think we really need to find an alternative option, so tell me something? Why can't we just saturate the complex with sleeping gas or something! Then go marching in through the front gates.' TA raised his hands in the air. 'Ahh! Hastings you're a complete genius, yes, we can drug the sea creatures beforehand, and when they are consumed by the Draco Claw then they will all be rendered useless.' Hastings raised his hand. 'Stop, please stop, right there, remember we are humans. It is much easier than that, I feel your alien ideology and strategy may fit well with an alien styled clandestine attacks and could very well work in principle, but I really think not in this case, and besides my best colleagues Darlene and Erica will go absolutely **apeshit** if I even attempt to offer them that fantastic but very unorthodox approach. But do, tell me something? This complex must have a waste recycle plant or a water outlet for used domestic water disposal? Surely, we can simply enter via the underground piping system.

I mean there must be a pipeline that services the base somewhere, that's surely a better option than being made into human fish paste before sunrise. Mind you though, we will need the drawings and plans of the DARPA layout. Can you get copies of them for us?'

TA then offered a strange smirk and responded. 'Are you sure that you want to go inside the **sewage and water systems**, how yuuuugh! We cannot do that, we the Igigi or the Anunnaki we are not designed to physically encounter human waste. The multitude of unknown toxins in your bodies would kill us within seconds. And you think travelling in a fish tank was pretty weird? You will have to go into this waste chamber without the presence of the Anunnaki or the Merlithian I am afraid. The germs and beasties in human bodily waste would rapidly attack our immune systems and remove us from existence. But if this is a real option for you humans to endure. Then be my guest, although you will have to find a way to gain us access as well, but, please only after you have showered and cleaned up of course.'

In reality, Kemp Hastings did not really relish at the thought of entering the sewage treatment system in the base either. But, he didn't exactly want to propose the plan to Darlene and Erica about fish tank services either for certain fear that his soft pink dangly parts would be ripped off and parting company with his person and quite literally hung out to dry! But it certainly would be the last place the Draco would look for any intruders. And the Draco species would never go anywhere near the human sewage treatment plant as they know that they themselves were as vulnerable to human waste as were the Anunnaki, nevertheless, Hastings and the girls could potentially don military style underwater scuba gear and remain quite safe if they could source some.

All Hastings had to do was convince the girls that it was one shitty option versus an aquatic one, and yet then again, he could also present the travelling fish tank option first. After a few more minutes of deliberation and chit chat the team then made their way deeper into the temple and found a spot in the crypt area to set up their command cell.

Chapter Twenty:

'An Freya' The Valkyrie Woman'

As Hastings ventured through the temple complex he entered the birthing chamber and sensed once again that the space was not void of either person or an entity, a living being was present, his hyper senses had been tweaked and his newly found sixth sense was certainly aware of an unnatural presence as the hairs stood up on the nape of his neck. As he momentarily closed his eyes he envisioned in his mind a single female figure, most certainly could be human. And from his inner sight line she was lying down in the **'Birthing bath'** but the bath was not empty but was full of a silvery shining almost transparent liquid. His impression was that this figure was semi submerged and was waiting for something to happen. He then grasped the Ankh staff firmly and waited patiently and then began stealthily and very cautiously edged his way along with his back against the walls towards the inner sanctum of the chamber. After a few painstaking minutes of moving around the cavern he physically spied the figure. It was certainly a woman and a most shapely attractive one at that. She was around six foot in height and clad in black leather robes topped off with a golden tiara that crowned her long blonde hair. Her arms were crossed over her chest and she carried the iconic symbol of the Ankh which was laid over the top of her golden breast plate. She was in every sense appeared to be warrior Queen.

The pool water had started to change in colour as he approached. The silvery aquatic gloop had started to sparkle and bubbled up with an emerald-green tint. As he gazed upon the woman her eyes opened slowly at first and her over-sized irises were bright blue with an ultra-white scilera which made Hastings take a deep breath and then he took a second glance. Then a voice broke the silence. It was a woman's voice, yet the lady was still submerged in the pool and was staring directly at him, although he could still hear her soft tones clear as day. Then the questions came.

'Who has evoked the triad?' Came the first question. 'And why have I been summoned here to this god forsaken rat pit of a planet?' Was the second question. Hastings remained very much silent and was aware that he himself was still a human hybrid Anunnaki figure but was humbled in the presence of the warrior visitor. Especially by the delicate sweet tone of her woman's dominating vibrating voice. It was clean, sharp, melodious and almost tuneful and was certainly in echo. It was verging on the mesmeric and hypnotic almost erotic frequency that shakes mortal man's sexual instincts. He then clasped his hands together then commented. 'Are you Hathor?' He asked and then waited for a response.

Then, there was a nanu second pause and a very awkward nothingness, and then the visitor sparked into life. 'You do not know who I am? But should know of my earthly presence and yet you ask me if I am some underworld entity that modern humans would call an ancient lady of the **ill reputed**, no, I am certainly not Hathor. But, I am An'Freya the Valkyrie Queen of the Norselands.' Hastings caught on very quickly and then almost apologised as he continued to engage the visitor.

'Queen An'Freya, you must forgive me, I am but a servant and messenger of the unknown, and, I do not know who has summoned your presence here to Egypt, but I do understand that the **Triad Lords** should never be disturbed, under any circumstances albeit, you must also understand that the great Lilith has commanded the Anunnaki to rise up and defeat a clutch of violent Draco Claw.'

There was a very distinctive electronic strike or flash in the chamber and Hastings had suddenly shot bolt upright. An'Freya slowly raised herself out of the pool and shook her head for a few seconds then stood fully upright as she spouted out a few more obscenities. 'Lilith you mean, Inanna, Ishtar, that underworld deceptive charlatan, the devil's little whore. The abomination who has been damned since the first day of man's creation. She is far worse than Hathor, no comparison there at all.' She said then continued whilst raising her voice a little louder. 'For the lust and sake of the angels in the heavens. Why have you sent me down here to this sordid place where only whores and the fallen are present.' And then she seemed to look upwards as if addressing some other entity in the room. After a few more seconds her outburst had stopped whilst addressing to the unknown gods above and stroked her breast plate with her hand. Hastings could not really answer her questions in any response or any conviction to her outpourings as he obviously understood that these underworld creatures of ancient time may well have a long history of anger and spitefulness between them, perhaps even an argument that could have originated and thus waited over thousands of years or more to come into the present to be resolved. Where entities could still be waiting to reconcile their differences. And like most modern women let alone underworld ones their memory was impeccable for **total recall** especially, more so, if they have held a certain grudge or had an ancient itch to scratch.

Which was more than obvious to be the case. Hastings then raised a hand to aid the entity out of the water. But he was far too late the Valkyrie Queen was already hovering a few inches off the dusty floor and hovering. He then moved to one side as the lady swept him by almost dismissing his presence as a mere inconvenience and then she settled down nearby the calling altar. After which she posed a few more questions. 'So where are we exactly? what is this dismal sanctuary? I have never liked Egypt.' Hastings gazed upon the Queen, acknowledging that she was even more erotic out of the water than she was submerged, however she certainly possessed a temper that mortal man does not want ever to experience. Well at least within his inner thoughts she was. Her ample breasts pushed forward through the golden under garment and he could not help himself staring again at the figure and was simply amused and almost aroused whilst staring at the Valkyrie Queen's beauty.

He then answered. 'We are located at Hathor, a Temple in the Dendera region within the old Anunnaki energy and vibration centre in Egypt, as you rightly guessed. And you have entered what is known as the Pleiadian **Birthing chamber**, from the underworld plain, I can only presume.' It was then that Hastings realized that the wrist band on his arm was glowing and vibrating. The Valkyrie Queen leaned over closer towards him and took a long sniff of the air around. 'I smell Anunnaki blood, but you are not of their species. You are a cross breed! my guess is that you are from the Davidic lineage of the Tribe of the Dan then you're a definitely a hybrid. And yet still dominant Anunnaki. What kind of trickery can this be? You have both the blood of the Anunnaki and the scent of the Albion King An'Tura, I can feel his vibration. It is all over you like a strange rash. This strain of lineage is not foretold in the Anunnaki legacy prophecy written by our ancients. You should not exist child of man. Can you explain yourself Adamite?' Hastings raised his staff off the floor and walked slowly to the left side of the Valkyrie Queen before offering her an explanation.

'Queen An'Freya. I am currently the Imperial Protector of the interred Anunnaki in Ahgartha, Antarctica, but am also told that I was the last line of human DNA hybrid now in the sixty-eighth generation and ancient line of core Anunnaki descendants. The breed that were originally spawned in Sumeria. And today, I remain within the colony in my human physical form here in the twenty first century. We have been sent here to Hathor by Lilith in order to engage with the Draco Claw and destroy their presence along with a clutch of Igigi people as the Claw have started a colonial war on earth and are trying to eradicate the Anunnaki hives.

'The Seed': 'Anu – Nexus'

The Valkyrie Queen then shook her head slowly from side to side then retorted. 'No, no, I don't agree with that at all, the Triad would never have been disturbed for such an insignificant event. There is an intergalactic disruption afoot, tell me Anunnaki Imperial protector where is she? Where is Inanna, that bitch Queen Lilith right now? I need her presence, summon her here at once, that is my command.' Hastings lowered his staff to the floor again, then bowed his head and spoke. 'Queen of the Valkyrie, I do not know how to summon Lilith directly as per your command, I understand that she may still be at Ahgartha.' She then replied. 'Mmm! Well, I can fix that, prepare yourself, Imperial Protector.'

The Valkyrie Queen walked slowly passed him and stared back again then spoke. 'Follow me, Adamite, we have to find the Phoenix cluster? It's here in this god forsaken place somewhere.' Within a few minutes having passed through three other chambers then having stepped into a small courtyard and ascended a few steps then through a few corridors An'freya suddenly raised her short golden Ankh and pointed it directly to the false doorway that sat a few feet above a carving of a Queen with four faces. Hastings had no idea which Queen but guessed It may have been Hathor's four face effigy depicting the four cardinal points of the compass. But, mostly by the look of disdain and almost hatred presented by An'Freya's facial expression.

'Give me your arm Adamite we have to function the zeta matrix. You must consume some of this heavenly dust.' She almost demanded. Hastings was bewildered then questioned the entity? 'Why should I consume this white powder.' He asked? An'Freya looked back at him in almost disbelief and appeared as equally bewildered as Hastings was. Then she explained. 'This is gold manna bread, it simply allows the physical realm to enter the ethereal realm in the heavens, or in this case the fourth plain.' Hastings then pursed his lips. 'Oh, that clears that issue up then.' An' Freya then placed her left hand over her own Ankh and reached out whilst flicking the golden wrist band on his arm. After a few seconds both Hastings and the Valkyrie Queen were gone in a flash. As he returned to his senses Hastings instantly grabbed at his Ankh staff having found himself back at the Habitat in Antarctica. But not quite in his physical form. The Igigi people in the laboratory had spotted the Valkyrie Queen's arrival and instantly fled the chamber, knowing full well that her raptor protectors would arrive shortly and most likely have them for lunch.

Hastings was then alerted to the presence of two of the biggest Harpy Eagle raptors known to the ancient world. He instantly recalled An Laara's very clear words of warning. '**Do not be in the presence of these beasts at any cost**' and as he was about to exit and flee the chamber in great haste was when the Valkyrie Queen raised her hand in the air and shouted. 'Stop! you son of Anunnaki - Imperial Protector, do not worry, nor flee from this place. My guardians are not hungry or they would have surely devoured your soul by now if they were, but, they are very fussy about who or what they eat! And besides you're a **Holo vibration and not very edible**.'

Hastings smirked and then joked. 'Well, I do hope they like squamate lizard steaks for lunch, because that's what will probably be on their next menu.' The Valkyrie Queen smirked and almost smiled in a very dismissive manner at his fleeting comments which were mostly triggered by sheer fright at the sight of the avians. An'Freya then moved towards the birds and started stroking each of their heads whilst playfully tweaking their beaks. The raptors seemed to **'purr'** not unlike a large domestic cat but more of a tiger or lion. Hastings then took three steps backwards and watched in amusement as An'Freya interacted with her heavenly guardians. It was then An'Freya proposed a response. 'My children, my protectors and my babies. These raptors are more loyal than most of the species I have encountered in many centuries of existence, and that includes the humankind beast. For my reasons only, I do not see the need to have your species ripped apart from limb to limb, spilling their blood everywhere. But especially more so now, well not you! because your human vibrations are all very different. They are not erratic as when most species meet or encounter my children are, and why you appear so calm and very collected is beyond my rational thinking. And yet you are not full Anunnaki either, all very strange to me. I will now meet with Lilith.' As Hastings remained in the chamber in his non-physical state An'Freya had sought out Queen Lilith and had engaged in her master plan. Hastings meanwhile was then interrupted by the motion of several light images that appeared between the illuminated walls and small pillars and were traversing the passageways that he had come to know so well in his previous exploits and visits to the Habitat's hibernation crypt. But these light columns were floating between a range of crystal upright epitaphs he had never seen before. He then reminded himself that he was not in the physical plain as he travelled from the phoenix house in Dendera and had crossed plains which logic says that he was in another world completely.

As he watched the seven small pillars of light enter a recess at the rear of the chamber. He followed after them. And, observed what they actually were, and most interestingly what were they doing. To his amazement he had entered into a fantastic panoramic abyss of lights and stars that sparkled brightly and seemed to stem into what he thought was the deeper heavens. Whilst viewing the spectacle he was captured in its rapture and was consumed by his own purple aura swirling around him finding himself to be in the presence of the

seven light columns that were forming and melding together into what was 'one' consciousness. Then he witnessed both An'Freya and Lilith facing each other and were each becoming entwined as they conversed. He saw many colourful sparks of light bouncing between the two, and every now and again a pulse of intense red light circled them causing both presences to raise their heads.

The surreal moments of this ethereal contact was away beyond any rational thoughts that he possessed. And he had made up his mind that, coming together in this way was probably how arguments or disagreements were played out and settled in the **'cell'** of the great arbitrator. It was only a short time before both Hastings and the Valkyrie Queen were sent back into the birthing chamber at Hathor.

Chapter Twenty – One:

'Encounter'

An'Freya had returned to the chamber at Dendera with the intention of understanding why her reanimation into the earth plain in this fourth dimension had been triggered. She was anxious to engage with the only other **underworld** entity in this domain that could shed any light on her predicament and provide the real answers on what was happening. Hastings meanwhile had sought out both Darlene and Erica in the lower crypt chambers and continued setting up the command cell.

As An'Freya emerged from the birthing temple doorway she was met instantly by an entity that stood fast and very dominating albeit, certainly appeared ready for war. The guardian was tall, almost seven foot in height with a sturdy physical frame and was dressed in golden robes that draped over her jewelled armour. The entity wore a golden crown of thorns at the base of her sun disk icon and held a crystal sword in her left hand. An'Freya remained unperturbed knowing full well that her avian raptors would soon join her and provide any security that she craved. All she would have to do was play for time as she engaged the temple Queen.

'**Hathor!** 'I see you are well overly dressed for the occasion, not really a surprise, very predictable just the same as that tramp Lilith was. Every day is a glorious festival day, but I must say it is **never a pleasure or** nicety to meet with any of you soul '**Enders'** you all seem to crave war and destruction and bring nothing but sorrow to the world around you. Yet! you party like there is no tomorrow, and you copulate as if there was going to be a moratorium placed on the use of the woman's womb, or worry that the charm of the vibrant rabbit season is coming to an end! But, yet you still exude and promote the important traits of deep love and acute affection to the many visitors that dare to tread within these very sinful walls. Tell me Hathor? Do you know why? have I been summoned here to this house of harlots, this hell hole of depravity?' Hathor the underworld sky goddess amongst many other astral disguises took a step forward and spoke very directly. 'An'Freya, firstly, let me remind you that you are in my domain, my house, my sanctuary,

'The Seed': 'Anu – Nexus'

my inner sanctum and not your so-called depraved house of harlots nor this hell hole that you imagine it be. This place An'Freya is the eternal home of the Pleiadian and, you of all the astrals should know more than most about the rules and the strict penalties for abusing them only too well. And just to let you know, I have imprisoned your big noisy parrots in suitable cages until we are finished with our business, smelly creatures that they are. 'I really do not know why you want these things around you in the physical plain. I mean why not get a golden phoenix or a young red dragon or even a lion or something that people can observe and admire. Why not find a Queenly animal that walks or accompanies you within the time dimension. Anyway, we cannot have them dropping their internal infested putrid waste and feathers all over the temple floors, as I have already said, you know the rules **'No pets'** in my house as Lilith has already discovered to her detriment bringing along that infernal Tiamat viper snake thing and that bloody Owl. So, shall we dispense with the unpleasant introductions and start again! Welcome to the House of Horus and the safe-haven of the Sun god Ra. You may bathe in the rich milky elixir of life at the 'Birthing chamber' if you do so desire, and feel free to dine on the succulent ambrosia fruit of the ancients with our eternal honeysuckle sap or drench yourself in the juices of our sycamore tree and of course, you may also indulge in the eternal seed of life from the gods or you may even wish to consume our honey cakes or 'manna-bread' where my servants will be at your command and call as you require.'

An 'Freya's eyes started turning to a bright firey red as her anger began to rage, she almost erupted but had contained her emotions. 'Do you think I was summoned here to have a bath and a wash, or eat your tarnished food or even indulge in your insidious sexual games? But, as much I would like to enjoy some of your hospitality Hathor, I feel, there is a deep albeit, very unnatural rhythm and disturbing vibration that is rippling across the frequencies of the heavens. Even this temple is pulsing with vibration and your four interlinked Keys of Nergal have been activated and they are pulsing away and coming into alignment. The zeta gateways have been opened again I can only assume.

We will have to make ready and expect the unexpected. These vibrations are occurring to such an extent that the council of five are very nervous indeed. We cannot endure another nuclear strike in the cosmos, and I can only surmise that the rising of the Triad is by design and may be imminent if Lilith's plan is not executed swiftly.' Hathor then stood fully upright and pouted her breasts outwards then swept her long golden robes around her waist and then sat down on the large crescent moon stone throne. Her crowned head dress depicting the cow-horns and the Aten sun disk encircled with a lashing of golden thorns began sparkling and lighting up against the bright lights within the chamber. In this supernatural hierarchy **state** of reality, signifies that Hathor was pretty much invincible against any dark influences generated from any of the twelve plains or circles of existence. She then spoke again. 'Yes, I can feel it too, the acute disharmony erupting around us is not what the Anunnaki want or need at this time, I also feel the presence of human hybrids who have arrived in this sacred place under the Anunnaki blanket of protection, but I do not know why? as there is also an ongoing integration with both the Pleiadian and Arcturian life forms. I have swept the lower chambers of this temple earlier this dawn and the power energy is certainly increasing. The great **'Pleaidian star chart'** was rotating in an anti-clockwise direction which can only mean one thing. Nibiru or Jupiter has changed their course and are heading back to Orion.' That surely cannot be right. As this will bring mass flooding and more magnetic disturbances leading to earthquakes and volcanic eruptions across this very planet. I have travelled between these boundaries of the heavens, and yet I feel no attraction of what links a new **trio or creation** together that serves any real Anunnaki purpose. Let alone anticipating the return or arrival of the planet Nibiru. I can of course confirm with you that we have indeed nurtured a hidden hive of Anunnaki, and perhaps the ancient Merlithian myth as far as the 4th plain is concerned is now in true existence.'

An'Freya answered her back with clear distinction. 'According to Lilith, I would gamble the heavens that the physical Merlithian have evolved and are being closely managed. And I know this can only be the clandestine work of her. Lilith will have a new clutch of offspring brewing in a womb somewhere. But, do tell me Hathor, what do think is going on with Mars? As I do not know the real reason why I have been resurrected?' Hathor smirked and watched An'Freya as she contemplated the rationale in her mind's eye as to why she was even at the Dendera Temple in the first place. An 'Freya' took two steps nearer to the seated Queen whilst taking in her splendid grandeur and her divine elegance along with her womanly charms as she spoke.

'You, Hathor, are the solar deity and the golden feminine presence of the divine entourage, surely, you must have an inclination of what is really going on with the council of five. Can you not ask your lords for an explanation as to what they are trying to achieve?' Hathor then smiled back at her with a very odd expression on her face then answered. 'We believe that the Draco are trying to rule the heavens again, and that is not really unexpected given their turbulent and violent history. And they will endeavour to disrupt both the longevity of the Anunnaki and gain their rightful place back in the heavens as they once did in the union with the early dominion.

And the fear in the council and the outer colonies is that the **Claw** will embark on another campaign of catastrophic destruction and could potentially succeed. Because, somewhere along the timeline they might have taken stock of the titan fuelled nuclear weaponry. Albeit, myself as the daughter of Ra, I cannot intervene directly as I have learned many lessons from my own turbulent past affairs and endeavours and not to get too involved, as I have been disciplined.

But I have obliged the Anunnaki to use my house across the 4th plain at this time. And, I have agreed that they can use the temple as their safe haven until they defeat the Claw and, then I can return back to the chaotic turmoil of the underworld. My own thoughts are that although **Lilith** has a grand plan. She is also very unpredictable and highly deceptive, perhaps you are simply here An'Freya to control her actions and ensure that we can maintain stability in the heavens and be warned that you may have to deal with her directly if she steps out of line.' An' Freya then responded. 'You have the power to control daylight. The lizard Claw hate the sunlight and they scour and hide at dawn. Maybe, you can intensify that solar 'light' around them and keep them underground and isolated then we can provide the Merlithian with support in order to hunt them down and succeed in their demise and eradicate their troublesome presence. Then I can turn my attentions to dealing with Lilith. You know only too well that the overlords Isis and Osiris would certainly approve of this strategic warring action against this enemy and to maintain control, although, we must tread very carefully.'

Hathor then responded. 'Just be very aware that Lilith is very deceitful indeed and most unpredictable as a very troubled soul, but I do not think she will remain on earth any longer than she needs to, as she still craves to master the Martian planet and procure a solid home base for the new Anunnaki legacy to continue. And she will have until I decide about providing that protection under the Eye of Ra to them. My true relationship with the Merlithian at the Sinia peninsula, if known is also no great secret and is good reason to presume that I have also served what I think is the hidden seed to this very day. As we once did for the early Pharaohs as they mined for our precious riches for the Anunnaki great purpose. And mankind, have been protected whilst working under the watchful eye of Ra by his omnipotent power in the new kingdom from their many enemies. But there is another warning for you to consider. We have unwittingly evolved the **Serpent line** and permitted them to break through our defensive net.

Which was not something that we had really anticipated. Their extradition has given them new purpose and subsequently triggered them to hide and construct a new plan to return to this plain and attack us from within, and now look at us. That serpentine ideology is raging through the Draco blood line and is coming back to bite us in the arse and they could well devour us in the process if they destroy the time construct! However, be very clear that if, we face the Draco, then we will be sure to meet the full wrath of the **Cobra Queen** head on. And if they raise any attack against the humans because as a species they are weak and vulnerable. Then, in order to preserve the word of the great '*Enki*' we must act decisively and very swiftly to protect humankind. Our greatest threat is that if the human's revolt to protect themselves from the Draco which is determined, then we must also consider that these hybrids may trigger another '**Mass nuclear event'** and we will all fall together.

We should consult further with the council?' Do we really know what they have in mind?' Hathor then stood up from her golden throne and stepped forward and whispered directly in her ear. 'All walls have ears, and all plains have eyes, we must settle our many differences quickly and lay them aside An'Freya, and ensure that Lilith does not betray the master plan. Because if we fail Enki and the Anunnaki in this issue then we may be seen to weak.

Then our expulsion from the **vibrational zone** will be swift and silent.' Hathor smiled then offered an option. 'An'Freya listen to me come take a rest, join me in the pleasures of this house and enjoy the vibrational rhythm of desire, immerse yourself in the elixir of life and drool on the fruits of the great lord Ra. And when the Aten sun arises we will strike at the Draco together.' Hathor then brushed down her long hair to one side and reached out and softly stroked the arm of An'Freya. The mistress of love and seduction may have just seduced another willing desirous partner in the house of ancient delights of the afterlife, albeit sitting within the fourth dimension in the Dendera domain.

And with yet another Queen at her side. It could also be said without question that the great **Queen Cleopatra** may have also enjoyed the more physical and sexual side of the Dendera temple whilst indulging in the fruits of human life that was on offer or that she had demanded. An'Freya, was momentarily mesmerised and began to swoon by her and almost seduced by Hathor's charms. Then she spoke again. 'So, tell me Hathor what if Lilith is successful? Are you saying that she will dominate the middle heavens and return back to the planet Mars. And maybe for all that could be a good thing, even more so if she remains out of our hair.' Hathor then answered. 'If the Anunnaki are supporting Lilith which they are, then of course you must also protect Lilith and the Merlithian in this grand quest at this time, because, if we do not, then the Claw will overthrow the Anunnaki. You know they are a spontaneous breed of unhinged reptilians and they don't think ahead as we do. But if they do choose to release these weapons of destruction once more into the middle cosmos then, we will witness complete anarchy again, and since you asked, about my perspective on things, then my answer to you is that it is more likely the real reason why you have been brought back into existence on this time plain.' An'Freya was nodding in agreement.

'Yes, that makes perfect sense now. An'Freya mulled over the invitation. 'Perhaps I shall dwell in the delights of your invitation here at Dendera for the time being, but, I shall return to Valhalla in the dawn mists and talk to the dimensional warriors and see what they have to say or to offer.'

After a short time in the Temple of eternal lust An'Freya returned to the birthing chamber then disappeared from the fourth plain.

Chapter Twenty – Two:

'The Hybrid An' Goose'

Reptile killer

Latin: *serpens*

The scientist An 'Laara had browsed the many animal species that were known to dwell across the planet earth, but, on this occasion she was seeking a beast that could be specifically DNA engineered for a very ad hoc purpose. And that purpose was to simply attack and destroy this breed of extra-large lizard snake hybrids that had recently became a significant enemy of the Anunnaki people. The space travellers of Niburu had reacted in such a manner to the Draco's warring tactics that the Anunnaki had tasked their chief bio genetic guru to find a **'killer solution'** in order to destroy the clutch of invaders that had penetrated mankind, and who were most certainly upsetting the proverbial Anunnaki apple cart in their turbulent wake, but the Anunnaki have designed a method to literally destroy their foe by direct animal DNA intervention. The African and Egyptian mongoose had been selected and An'Laara had chosen wisely mainly due to the amazing unique DNA defence mechanism towards the volatile and deadly **'spit'** of the King Cobra. She had decided that out of the thirty or so other species on offer she had selected the wee beasties to hybridise with correctly. Which were exactly what she had in mind. This mongoose breed was deemed the better choice from all the other vicious beasties that could potentially be exploited as good candidates and were destined to become beasts that could attack an **alien 'lizard or snake entity'** and easily win by using the animals robust defence system that was already in place.

Thus, deemed the animal as the ultimate choice in a defensive measure providing a predictable outcome for the demise of the 'Claw'. It was almost the same poetic ideology that the Anunnaki and the council of five had employed whilst targeting the Draaken King in an earlier encounter and had formed the hybrid Honey Badger and Hyena project. The current plan was to create a modern hybrid specimen between a long-haired hyena and the humble but vicious Egyptian mongoose. Presenting yet another unique new species into the human food chain. The end-result being a four hundred pound, five - foot tall, long haired half hyena and half mongoose carnivore combining both viciousness and strength together that can deal effectively with any onslaught when the need arose. The scientist was also aware that scavenger hyenas are known for their intense squealing and loud night howling and perhaps these predators were more akin to the feline of the species as opposed to that of the male carnivorous variety of breeds that we know of today and out of the four common hyena breeds the hyena have evolved in differing habitat preferences, as an example the **Aardwolf** which lives in dry, open bushland and desert plains. Whereas, the **Spotted and Striped hyena** choose to live in the more mountainous regions surrounded by heavy woodlands.

The ***Brown haired Hyena,*** on the other hand is more of a nomadic creature which was specifically targeted as the beast inhabits the vast plains and sandy arid deserts of the planet and have been known to scavenge in dense urban areas which also makes them a menace to the human population. An'Laara also deduced that each beast was built slightly different in their bodily make up and no two creatures are actually identical.

Albeit, their skeletal structure differed slightly with a short torso and low hindquarters but with the larger breeds possess a more powerful and very pronounced jawbone that can snap the bones of a man in half with just one swift snap. The species in general have long forelegs and thick necks with rough matted and rugged fur which runs from their heads to their tails and where their backbone slopes noticeably downwards. From her studies the scientist understood that the standard mongoose could kill a king cobra in a pitch battle whilst being protected from the snake's toxic venom. She had also thought it worthy of note to mention that the mongoose could also engage with the deadly black mamba snake or an inland taipan or even a small python and survive. The Black Mamba as further example as it is found today is the second-longest venomous snake after the King Cobra. They are both known for their large size, quickness, agility and extremely potent venom, making them two of the deadliest snakes in the world.

However, the Anunnaki bio-scientist had created a creature that would simply fight off and defeat the common brown bear if need be, and snakes and lizards of the larger persuasion were not going to be an issue. The blending of these two incredible breeds would firstly feed the animal's natural instinct of attacking and devouring cobra snakes, crabs and small lizards in an instant. The difference being the lizards and snakes in the mind of the Anunnaki were going to be certain giants of their species. The required profile of the new beast would certainly have more weight, agility, cunning and greater speed. And this breed unlike the common mongoose could never be tamed for domestic purposes and if not controlled correctly may introduce an even greater threat to mankind hence, why An 'Laara was introducing an in-built safety mechanism that would enable the Anunnaki to render the beast inert when required. The scientist also chose to colour the DNA samples with the lighter brown striped and spotted appearance giving them a hint of desert camouflage. From the sample of the young Hyena currently in captivity (laboratory) she had recorded as to how their howling almost **'laughing'** cries sent a cold fear and uncanny vibration across the room and she instinctively knew that the Draco would almost shiver in fear on hearing theses desperate haunting shrieking cries.

An'Laara eventually dwelled on the fact that she could also be unleashing an incredibly intelligent animal into the world and paused for thought to the extent that she may be creating a creature twice as toxic as the Draco themselves, but certainly not as intellectual. The specimen in the laboratory was soon to be released back into the wild as an **apex predator** but not without inserting a positioning chip in her hide to locate her whereabouts and her new laboratory designed offspring at any one time. And as expected she also had a womb full of little **Mongoose and Hyena monsters that she had tagged as (An'Monyena**) that would soon be born and endure an accelerated rate of growth .

The scientist then wrote a few notes in her diary:

The chosen mongoose specimens are one of at least four known mammalian taxa with mutations in the nicotinic acetylcholine receptors which simply protects the beast from snake venom, where in reality, it inhibits the venom from binding together. Therefore, in order to control the beast we shall introduce a composite glycosylation, which is the presence or absence of glycosyltransferases, which dictates **which blood group** *the antigens are presented to as a host or target, in this case we shall target 'R' Type blood groups (Positive and Negative) and this immunological role will drive changes in the glycan heterogeneity state thus creating a barrier or an enticer as a zoonic virus. I have introduced a high frequency* **plasma burst bubble** *into the bloodstream that will erupt at the given frequency and burst the four heart chambers of the animal if desired.*

The direct intervention for human controls will be the same method by employing a controlled burst bubble approach which is designed to be similar as to how the Anunnaki deal with any living creature but more specifically.

'The Seed': 'Anu – Nexus'

The purple blooded human rulers who will be removed using blood antigens to stem their natural progression. The Anunnaki scientists will have the opportunity to repeat the process against the cross breed of the mature Herpestes-Hyaena with an upgraded antigen and the creature will be known as an (**An'Goose**).

An additional known fact about the mongoose presently is that it is a fairly intelligent animal, whilst also being tagged as one of the most dangerous of animals on the planet having eradicated a complete species of both rats and vermin colonies within their own local habitats. But this new creature would be taught to hopefully avoid or evade the **Igigi and the human species**, and of course it's handler and designer An 'Laara. The average mongoose today has a long face, small round ears and long tapering nails with non-retractable claws and is pretty much a solitary animal. Unlike the new hybrid mongoose with greater predatorial aspects of an unhinged raptor. However, it may be common knowledge that an eagle or buzzard would normally attack larger carnivores such as a wildcat or fox in the cycle of life or the food chain and would certainly attack the humble mongoose without question.

But the new Anunnaki breed of mongoose hybrid is something entirely different. An Laara had also studied the mongoose in fine detail before deciding on the unique DNA recipe for a beast that would become top of the food chain instantly, suffice to say that the Draco Claw species are in for quite a shock if, and when, they are confronted by this new age hairy demon from the laboratory universe. And it is with no surprises we may find that the Raptors - Harpy Eagles also have a new food chain species **counterpart** to contend with. The only fear was that the new creature could attack and kill An'Freya's valuable pets. This event would wreak a certain havoc amongst the Anunnaki. All An'Laara had to do was to work out a plan to ensure that both the new age Hyena and An Freya's Raptors would never come into direct conflict with one another.'

Chapter Twenty - Three:

'The theft of the Covenant Star Stones - Axum'

The village of Axum in Ethiopia had been less busy over the last few weeks and was generally bustling with the constant trail of visitors that had taken a pilgrimage to be in the same location of the unworldly 'Ark of the Covenant' a religious icon that was so well recorded in biblical history that it really cannot go unnoticed. And, the visitor season was soon coming to an end.

The current Guardian Elijah had awoken early in the morning and had enacted his daily security routine of walking within the shrine and ensuring that all in the house of God was in good order as he had done for many years as had his forefathers before him. As he walked within the tabot chamber he acknowledged that it was unusually quiet and seemed much colder. But, he was simply astounded to find that the holy Ark in the calling chamber was sitting **open** and an incredible light shone out from within the relic container. As Elijah shielded his eyes from the intense glare of the penetrating light he was suddenly overcome by a bout of an incredible vibration that coursed through his spine and rattled his bones to destruction to the point where he fell down on to the solid cold stone flooring and was quite dead. Having been literally shaken to death.

In the history that follows this great icon of worship many devotees have died at the awesome power of this relic and Elijah had just become another modern statistic lured into a high volatile environment by his holy drive to serve his purpose on earth under the watchful eyes of his overlords. The ancient overlords who most likely understood radio-active poisoning and the realms of vibration. The Arch deacon of the Eritrean Orthodox church was the man who oversaw the daily support and protection of the Mary of Sion church and normally made a twice daily journey from his nearby home to the shrine. With his visits in the early morning and last thing in the evening, then his eternal task to serve his god was done, and after which he could rest having made visual contact with the Guardian. But for some unknown strange reason he had also awoken away too early with a strange chronic uneasiness in his mind that something was not right in the small village. His gut instinct told

'The Seed': 'Anu – Nexus'

him to visit the shrine soonest to remove any fears, worries, concerns, anguish and suspicions that he might have held and lay them to rest.

As he waited at the perimeter gate entrance, he had observed that the main central door was still closed and that the external long colourful linen drapes had not been set to one side as an indicator that all was well within the building. The Arch Deacon shouted three times to Elijah, but his callings received no response. He then left the immediate area and summoned the Royal courtiers and Church leaders together and informed them of his findings. A great sense of panic had set into the knot of clerics and the senior Bishop of the Eritrean Orthodox Church had permitted the use of a **small drone** to be employed immediately to take a glimpse inside the holy shrine.

The operation was conducted after a strict rule was imposed over the village of Axum where all telecommunications and internet links were immediately 'cut off' and the Church leaders had decreed that no people were permitted to be within one kilometre of the shrine's location as the clandestine operation took place.

The secret drone footage was to be reviewed by only two church leaders and their sense of loss was quite obvious as they watched the drone fly around within the shrine. The chamber itself lay undisturbed but the 'Ark' was sitting in its normal position apart from the fact that the ancient animal skins and drapes were currently lying on the floor.

Had Elijah lost his senses and tempted his fate, and had he disturbed the Ark? at this juncture, no one really knew apart from the Guardian himself, And the **'Mercy Seat'** itself was seen to be hovering about one metre from the top of the Tabot holder's shoulders held in suspension by some great unforeseen force with what appeared to be a modern gyroscope spinning on its axis in the middle space. The illumination from within the Ark was very intense and at times prevented the drone camera to take any real time clear footage, but it was obvious to the observers that something strange had occurred and poor Elijah the last guardian still lay motionless on the floor.

It was at that point he was the only one who could explain the goings on in the chapel through the night as the world of Ethiopia lay asleep. However, as the church elders and leaders spent their time watching the 'live' drone in operation they had observed what was occurring and were distraught. However, there was something strange still in the small chamber. A green misty haze was building up and the shadow of a humanoid figure appeared to be flirting back and forth across the camera lens through the glaring light. The drone operator struggled to keep track of what looked like a figure of a person as it flirted back and forth. As the keepers watched the recording the footage momentarily paused for about six seconds then restarted and the clerics witnessed the actual raising of the mercy seat as it raised even higher obviously assisted by this alien unseen force. It could only be described as anti-gravity at work as no physical apparatus was present, however just nearer toward the end of the recording a single image of a tall shape was visible at the East end of the chamber and appeared to be that of a humanoid figure not unlike a large serpent head on a man's body and was in full view for several seconds, Albeit, the entity was facing the actual Ark. Then the footage stopped again and then the equipment simply ceased to function.

No less than four minutes had passed after the recording was finished when there was a very distinctive lightning strike over Axum and three heavenly highly charged electric bolts of lightning shot out of the morning sky and struck the holy church icon and its surroundings, almost setting fire to both the foliage and the rooftop itself. Then the rains fell from the heavens.

A huge sense of panic had settled in with the local population and there was a single report from the military onlookers that a strange silver oval shaped flying craft had been observed nearby one of the huge obelisks that lay four hundred feet away just seconds after the drone had ceased working. The Church Clerics were now in complete turmoil.

Had they just witnessed an ungodly or inexplicable event within their holy shrine and they were obviously shocked especially having maintained the Ark's physical security for the best part of a thousand years plus. And yet what was the status of the Tabot now! Had it been damaged or worse had their god retrieved the artefacts that were secured within the Ark from ancient days. Or had an entity been visiting the chamber to check on the management of the holy relic. Questions? Questions? Questions? The answers of which now only sat with the Draco Claw species.

After the holy ritual of extraction was completed and Elijah's body had been retrieved by employing the ancient golden tether ritual step by step. And thankfully as a devout guardian poor Elijah had himself ensured that the ritual procedures had been followed to the letter of the divine law and was in tether having tied the golden rope around his waist as he traversed the inner sanctum. Within hours of the unnatural event, the Orthodox leadership had installed a replacement Guardian in the holy building as not to alert the local population that their beloved and precious relic had either been compromised or had been tampered with and that Elijah was in fact dead due to natural causes, just like his predecessors.

Chapter Twenty – Four:

'Bio Geometry'

The Merlithians had eventually arrived at the temple of Hathor and met with TA and Hastings within the central large hypostyle multi columnated structure. Hastings and the girls were making ready for their trip to the Americas when An'Mer entered the chamber and conveyed his latest information to the team. 'We have just heard from the Pleiadians that the Draco have removed the 'Star Stone' and the snake staff of Aaron from the Axum Hive. The Ethiopian church are not exactly overly excited nor impressed at the prospect of telling their people that their holy relics have gone missing. I suppose their only comfort will be that the Levite monks will have to explain to the masses that the star people have returned to claim their property.'

Erica turned around from her friends and faced An'Mer then spoke. 'So, what does that mean for the Arcturians and the Pleiadians?' An'Mer leaned forward and placed his knee on the floor and faced her before offering any answer. 'Well in real terms Erica it means that the Draco are trying to gather all the keys of Nergal together, which could prevent any species from stopping them in this madcap drive to command the planets by posing a certain nuclear threat, most likely finding a way to destroy us all. The Star Stones together are the central energy force that harmonises the outer colonies, and if the Draco Claw can control one planet then they will eventually destroy all the other planets including the Pleiadians and the Sirian ones and any other colony that are too advanced for them to control. And thus, bring the remainder into servitude.'

Erica nodded her head in acknowledgement then responded again. 'So, this is about planet domination in this context of war and overthrow, and really not that much different from the original Anunnaki dominion legacy plan here on Earth.' An'Mer nodded his head and closed his eyes and simply could not answer the question with any real conviction, and found himself at an awkward point in the conversation, as they engaged with one another. Hastings sensed the heightened tension between the two in the air and quickly but strategically intervened. 'Erica, An'Mer, I have some points for you both to consider. The reason the Anunnaki came to earth in the early years was - yes! to source a new workforce and - yes! to create and evolve the hybrid colonies of many countries to succeed as miners as were the Igigi people. And from that point onwards things had progressed quite well. The people or new breed of people were not exactly slaves but a force that was fed, watered and catered for. But unlike the Anunnaki, the Draco intend to simply destroy all the inhabitants of the planets before considering anything else. Whereas, the Anunnaki had developed early mankind to where we find ourselves today. And more importantly, if they had not then we would simply not exist either.

What is happening currently is that the Draco Claw are repeating their own history and trying to attempt what is called a '**Grand reset'** and remove both humans and Anunnaki from existence. The subtle difference being that modern day humans still possess twenty percent of the Anunnaki DNA blood line in their make-up and the Draco should really be seen as an invading toxic virus that wants to poison mankind.'

An'Mer looked at Hastings in an entirely new light. It was then that An'Lara had slowly stepped forward and then intervened. 'I sense a negative vibration in the air, I can feel a cold presence in this temple, and it is rapidly moving within the lower complex.' The chamber at that point began to fill with light green mist and Hastings felt the atmosphere change to an electric almost caressing pulse of energy and knew that his recent acquaintance the Norske Queen An 'Freya was nearby, as he could also sense and smell the presence of the two vicious raptors that he had been exposed to earlier. And may just have come through on the physical plain.

But understood they should not be at Hathor but should be ripping out in Valhalla somewhere. Which made him feel very uneasy regarding the presence of both Erica and Darlene. He then motioned the girls to the far Eastern corner of the chamber and passed the Ankh staff over to Erica. 'Stay here and do not attempt to go anywhere near the central part of the chamber or those birds under any circumstances. It is not evil that we face here, but raw animal existence and they might be bloody hungry. An 'Freya has two very large protectors in the form of these two carnivore raptor Harpy Eagles and they are not thinking type of birds of prey if you get my drift.'

Darlene responded. 'So, what do we do with this Ankh?' Hastings smiled back at her and commented. 'Absolutely nothing, unless they attack you of course, then you hit can hit them on the head, these birds are simple killers, I am working on the hunch that since An 'Freya has already introduced me to the raptors my logic says that I am no threat, but I am not sure if they are going to be here in the physical or ethereal, apparently you can never tell with An'Freya.'

Darlene smiled and commented. 'How do you know this Kemp? But, honestly is that wise to really assume such a dumb thing, I mean good luck with that one, you certainly have more faith than I do. Hopefully your thinking logic pays off.'

Hastings answered. 'It's a long story Darlene but trust me, I am pretty sure I will be safe.' Erica and Darlene then watched on in silence and moved back into the shadows as Hastings returned to the main group of aliens. It was then that An'Laara spoke with him directly. And this was now the second time in her three thousand years of existence she had engaged directly with a human.

'I presume the Arcturian and the Pleiadian do not experience heightened vibration and rhythms the way the female Anunnaki do?' The Imperial Protector clasped his hands and responded out of politeness. 'No. you are quite correct they don't but, sort of do, although not in the sense that they can interpret direct vibration and can see patterns and visualise in their minds a being or a shape as clear as you do. As we are not gifted with the core feelings of true spirit energy. But we do possess an impeccable and very uncanny sixth sense. And the female understanding of the vital life forces are clearly understood of both the physical human vibrations and the heavenly scalar wave patterns or chi, like the ones we experienced earlier when Hathor had broke the 4th plain. Suffice to say An'Laara when the human female intuition is tweaked, they are pretty much on point. They do not or cannot dwell on the singularity theory or indeed the multi polarity of balance. But they do understand the hallmarks of vibrational gold and some of the crystal signals and possibly they might be able to interpret some of the hermetic series of alchemy equations to a fair degree, but anything above four of the twelve bands is beyond the human hybrid intellect.

Especially regarding multiple levels and plains as what you actually deem as the science of Bio Geometry or real visions.' An'Laara smiled again.

'So much development for our children that still needs to take place.' Hastings tapped the side of his head with his forefinger then responded very politely. 'You can take on that mammoth task later, once we get out of this charade and when we all have more time to spare.' After their meeting both Erica and Darlene left the chamber and proceeded down into the crypt area of the Temple knowing that the tall beings would not venture near them due the restrictions and space of the small tunnels within the lower enclave of the structure.

Kemp meanwhile remained in the birthing chamber and was working out what he thought would be a course of action, having listened to An' Freya who had explained that the Norske entities did not appear to be too worried about the Draco's impending attack, but highlighted that they would be watching over Dendera more closely.

Chapter Twenty - Five:

'Fly with me'

An'Mer had sat down beside Hastings after the meeting with An'Freya and learned that the Norsk entities deemed this event to be too trivial for them to break their code of existence but had indicated that the An'Tura king would be taking stock of any middle earth disruptions that the 'Lithith' could inflict on the heavens if she was successful in reaching Mars.

An'Mer was unusually calm and almost accepted the fact that humans are very instrumental in the longevity of the modern Anunnaki and had decided that more information would be imparted to the imperial protector at a later time. An'Mer then discussed the key elements as to why the Anunnaki had evolved in the middle east with their planned transport routes in and out of the continent. As they both conversed Hastings had sampled the glass looking alcohol grapes and had found them quite intoxicating as had An'Mer himself and they consumed a fair few as they bonded.

The Merlithian then sat on the floor which was a posture that the Anunnaki deemed almost as subservient then spoke. 'So' here is what I think, I can tell you about the movements of our craft across the skies and the surface of earth, and I will try and explain why this was the reason important enough **not** to fly here to Egypt directly from Antarctica. The main technical reason was that the Draco would determine our flight plan in advance and, then simply intercept our craft just as swiftly as swatting a fly. Although unlike above surface flying at more than thirty feet we are visible to technology, although using the NTLM markers - **Near to Land Mass** which masks the actual magnetic signature from smaller craft are hidden. We could be cloaked or hidden, but only if we move between eight and twenty-two foot above ground level, then the craft become blind to radar. Albeit, anything flying higher than that and the radar would target the signal.

In times gone by the Anunnaki primarily employed the '**Landing grid' theory** which encompassed the key natural mountain peaks of the Eastern regions and their magnetic signatures as direction markers. Which are ironically the same word in our language as in your speech patterns, it is what we call Pyak or **'Peak'** also, as reference points, and the 'Giza' complex was one of three hundred and twelve structures that had to be synthetically built to accommodate **'Air to land'** movement and support the telemetry radiowaves and location beacons within their design. The three peak mountains for this zone are **Zion, Ararat and Zephim** which all hold self-management systems or (remote stations), and they are also managed by the Pleiadians from the Skylink network when required.

The great part of this program was that your earth has a huge magnetic central belt that is four hundred miles wide and around thirty five thousand miles long and actually traverses back and forth across the entire surface of the planet like a maze of avenues, and these lines move and alternate slightly every day. We have used the mountain what you humans call mount **Ararat** as the primary route 'peak' into the Sinai peninsula. Although you must understand that there is a similar mountain range that is captured in Saudi Arabia which was used as a default peak. And from there on in we could land at any of the receiving ports along the great 30th parallel.

Giza was once the main command hub and these are real spaceports that you humans seem to have an issue of understanding as to their real functionality. The reality is that when any earth human aircraft move along these known **'charged landing grids'** they simply suffer acute magnetic interference and their aircraft instruments simply stop functioning as the power grid is of a very high resonance and impact the crystals within human archaic craft that simply melt or burn out, and cannot cope, even over water they may fail to function.

The snow peeked caps in the tundra on the other hand, sit at around five thousand one hundred meters plus above sea level and other mountains are actually submerged underwater. Again the example being that mount Ararat which is ideal for us as the huge rocky outcrops retain volcanic naturally occurring radio-active material (NORM) or residue, constantly spouted out by the weeping mountainous inverted cones.

And you need to understand that the elements of height, density and radio waves can create a real **concern** if we suffer any meteoric anomalies or even lightning strikes in the regions that we fly across, and our craft have been known to crash land. And probably why a couple of extra-terrestrial aircraft have lost control and were downed by your mother nature.

We also define this place Ararat as a **'port entrance'** in our records. As does human history reflect whilst referring to the ark of Noah and the holy mountain, a known Anunnaki landing point. We the Merlithian relate to this place as San Katerina. So, as an example, if you were flying from Orion to

Giza you would follow the **interceptor guiding beacon signals** which are very recognisable physically due the size of the **obelisks** that are attached to them and as you fly over them, they simply update your location. There are other power beacon houses that also include larger multi stage or step construction structures, as is found at the (Saqqara pyramid), which was mainly designed for landing heavier trade craft to touch down on earth. And our very heavy air freighters require extra upward magnetic push from the generator complex to cushion the magnetic squeeze before their actual touching down.

Not unlike the old Ziggurats of Babylon that would often crumble under the stress and weight if heavier craft attempted to land there, because their vibrations would increase the structures stress points to breaking point. And that pressure was too much for granite stonework to endure and would crack and disintegrate under the shear weight of the craft.

The walls of Jericho and the keys of Nergal (the Ark - Star Stone scenario) is a similar example but on a much smaller scale. One important factor to consider is that **line of sight** around the pyramids is also significant and a craft could only land at **'Apex'** times. This meant that the pilot would have to observe the line of the shadows or the great silhouette of the pyramid as they approached before landing their craft, because if they landed their craft incorrectly then the charging gyroscopic cells in the craft would not fully regenerate or not fully recharge after touch down. Thus, not being ready for their next journey, as it would be off centreline. The Giza limestone build was an Anunnaki state of the **art invention** for this very purpose, and even in darkness of the night the craft could land more easily due to clear visibility and their orientation, and of course the pyramids would shine like a huge sun mountain on approach under - **ultra violet light.**

And a concept that all Anunnaki craft have fitted by default. Often pilots would request early landings and follow the **sundial method** for ease of landing at Giza during daylight, which was basically instrument free as the crew would know what actual time of the day it was by the length of the shadow cast over the plateau. And land their craft using the huge shadow 'arrows' as indicators of point. Especially more so, as they arrived from the East via Baalbek in Lebanon and then head across the mountains which were quite literally their guide.'

Hastings raised his hand and asked a question. 'An'Mer are all these space ports driven by one command cell or are there several little command centres?' An'Mer clasped his huge hands together then spoke in a fairly quieter tone as he picked another alcohol laced grape from the ever serving

'The Seed': 'Anu – Nexus'

decanter. '**Ararat**' is the only real command centre within the earth plain, a central hub if you like. The one location that can either activate or deactivate the many location beacons that serve to guide all craft on direct demand. There is another off-planet hub which is on Orion and that is a bit more complex to explain than that of Giza.

When you approach from the South Eastern side of the desert on earth you will pick up the '**Shumar** ' mountain peak, which is a pivotal anchor point 'cross-path' that either directs you to either Giza or on to Antarctica. We at Katerina can disrupt this route if and when we need to especially as the Draco try to start any air movement outside the DARPA complex in Nevada, where we just simply re-align the beacons and hide the real location in geographical terms which, the travel data will be mixed up. And the Draco will become confused and most certainly lost.

But only for a short period of time. Therefore, in order to do this, we must also destroy or disable the synthetic Obelisk at where the humans call their **Whitehouse** in America first, and this should prevent the Draco engaging with earths elite Igigi directly. Because they won't be able to find them or direct a communications signal to them, well at least not electronically.

But before you depart on our quest we must provide you and the girls with 'Shakra belts' These are total body wraps that carry the elements of the vibrational shakra and they wrap around the body like a membrane harness and then fuse with your own spinal tissue, providing the wearer with a sort of protection against negative or blocking vibrational energies whilst heightening the actual body frequency to receive specific vibrations.

These spinal webs, align the mind of the human and the core Anunnaki together. These are simply a modified version to fit the dimensions of your human spinal cord that taps directly into your subconscious. Not to worry though they only tingle when primarily activated and a high frequency will stimulate your human synaptic nerves in a milli-second, we have these in our natural DNA, but An'Laara says that they will not harm the human body in any way. This skeletal Shakra belt will give you more power and energy when you get excited or have to engage with an enemy.

Here remove your robe and I will demonstrate how it works.' Hastings stopped and grabbed An'Mer's arm. 'Are you sure these things are safe.' An'Mer sort of smirked then spoke. 'We are Anunnaki we don't do uncalibrated risk, because these are a mesh tissue you wont even know you are wearing it.

Your skin tissue will simply absorb the shakra and a zillion stimulated nanu nerve stems will connect together and voila you are done.' The Anunnaki warrior then placed the thinner than thin artificial membrane tissue across the back of Hastings who momentarily shivered and tightened up as the membrane gripped his skin and was instantly absorbed. After several seconds Hastings looked up at An'Mer and reached out to grab his arm again.

Hastings then tried to grip his right hand and found to his amazement that on contact he felt as though he had known An'Mer all his life. It was a synthetic and highly technical Anunnaki 'bond' that neither of them could really understand, especially after the best part of at least three thousand years of separation, but An'Mer realised very quickly that the power in the human's grip was almost as equal to his own and he flinched slightly. He even contemplated for a few seconds that Hasting's intellect would be also accelerated.

'It is done, I feel you have no conception of what your bloodline really is, and this membrane has actually done the trick for you, and look, you are much stronger now and over time you will start to think like us, welcome the Anunnaki construct.' So let me recap for you, firstly the Sinai control centre is operational for now, but we have left a little surprise should the Draco try to make any adjustments to the technical systems manually,

An 'Greggar has designed a remote control - function, I have no idea what it does or how it works, so we need to ensure that An' Greggar remains safe at all times. Another part of this conundrum for humans is the '**charging source or power key**' or the 'tablets' what the Anunnaki call the keys of Nergal, which are simple power grid cells. There are four of which are located here in this Complex at Dendera, they are actually secondary cells but will assist us. These are secreted into the walls at the lower chamber of Hathor's oracle, and they will be contained in heavy granite or gold boxes where their power can be kept stabilised.

I understand that the keys are also '**technical brains**' and communications pods for nuclear impulse energy. And that is what the Draco are trying to gather together, and we know that the temple in Ethiopia is just one example of where parts of the master keys are located.' Hastings shook his head.

'You know the human race will go absolutely bananas if they ever learn that any one of these objects has gone missing from one of their temples. I mean biblically the people will simply commit suicide or start great world wars in response and despair will reign high.' An'Mer almost smiled.

'Don't you worry about that for now we have that in hand, when we retrieve the keys of Nergal from the Draco you can return them to their rightful place in Axum. But first, we have to acquire them.' But please be mindful this is not just a radiation source. These cells will allow us to talk directly with the Draco and we can therefore, manipulate them, but only if we are clever enough. Although to do this we must also travel to **Baalbek in the Lebanon** to the ancient temple of the stars at Heliopolis, where we make contact the Draco first through the earthly **vibration cords**, as per Lilith's instructions. I think she will want to engage with Shamgaz and provide an option to stand down and return to the Andromeda belt, if he chooses not to, then the powers of the universe will strike without question and with no compassion.

The Baalbek complex houses natural vibration centres as does Hathor that can literally pick up the multitude of frequencies of the **holo keys** as they bounce around the stonework and they actually sit along these underground energy ley lines I mentioned earlier, they are located below many ancient flight paths or air tracks that we don't use anymore, mainly due to this anomaly. It will be the lowest form of frequency that the human contact centre at NASA /SETI and the project **'Listen'** command team can tune into when we require them to, and the Draco most likely will already be in communication with them through the corrupt Igigi.' Hastings drew some time and thought for a while then removed his little red book from his pocket and opened it up. Then located an ancient script he had once copied. It read:

- *A message is sent from heaven*
- *It is heard in Heliopolis*
- *And it is repeated in Memphis by the fair of face*
- *It is composed in a despatch by the writing of Thoth*
- *With regard to the city of Amen (Thebes)*
- *The matter is answered in Thebes*
- *A statement is issued and a message sent to?*
- *The gods are communicating using transponders*
- Remember the sphinx feet are radio beacons? (Hastings)
- Between the feet the extension cords dwell.
- End text. Ancient statement pre anti diluvian

'Well! said Hastings 'That certainly covered a few things I certainly did not fully understand.' An'Mer, then the giant stood up towering over Hastings, he made a final statement. 'We are not that far apart in our worlds and we are bonded with our distant blood, there are no other humans like you, as you can imagine, I was never going to understand this predicament but my mother was clear about her expectations, and I will honour them' He then walked through the great halls and found the Merlithian and was intercepted by TA.

Chapter Twenty – Six:

'Intercept'

TA had entered the chamber in a bit of a frenzy, almost panic stricken and informed the team that the Draco communications had been intercepted and that the Claw were planning to flee earth and take control over the Hive on Mars soonest. An'Mer had stood fully upright. 'This cannot be allowed to happen we must intercept the Claw immediately and prevent any further intervention with the Mars Hive, if they work out that the weapons are not there and can identify anyone that knows where they are located, and that includes Lilith then they will simply destroy the whole place. That incursion will bring a certain disaster.'

Hastings had entered the chamber again and faced An'Mer and presented a quick plan. 'An'Mer we know that this Shamgaz may well be one of the breed that have taken over DARPA, and his counterpart will be on Mars awaiting instructions. I suggest you get us a flying craft that can take myself and the girls to the Americas where I can destroy or at least knock out the **Obelisk** in Washington, if I can do this swiftly. Then you will have a bit of time to concentrate on the Mars side of the attack and deal with the Claw up there.' As he pointed to the heavens.

'They won't be expecting any trouble or to warn the corrupt Igigi at DARPA of their plans. Then after which we will go directly to DARPA and engage the rogue elements of what is left of the Draco. And when you return we will start our assault. I am sure that, they are still evolving, unless they are already mature. I will not be alone though as we can bring TA along as support, and of course An'Nanu's and An'Laara's hybrid beasts will be present for our protection. And if we are successful in entry to the base laboratories then we can destroy the incubation chambers and the science labs.'

An'Mer nodded. 'That was not exactly what I had in mind, but, time is now critical, it all makes logical sense. And if this is successful, then we could move the existing weapons to Orion where the overlords will protect them. But, I will need to talk with Lilith first.' Hastings then left An'Mer to his own devices and gathered the girls together and offered the two amazing scenarios as to how to gain entry into DARPA military test base whilst explaining that things had changed and the Claw were starting to move with haste, but, neither strategies were going to be easy options to present to the two most cynical people he knew.

Darlene and Erica to say the least both instantly rejected, dismissed, cast aside, dispelled, threw out, binned and cast away with conviction or did not even consider any option about sharing a fish tank with creepy sea creatures, and that much Hastings knew was going to be their final answer. Although, oddly enough during their 'tet a tet' Erica saw the logic in entering the camp employing the underground piping systems and had quite literary convinced Darlene that it was probably the only safest route to take and that would lead them into the centre of the base.

The notion of walking into the camp through the sewage output utility according to her was not going to be an issue as the environmental protection laws of the land even for the military machine followed very strict governmental guidelines rules and bye laws about handling human waste in any community and, stated that all primary piping was to be sealed and flushed within a closed loop system.

But there were also the services common manifold pipework array that was about fifty inches in diameter that provided the domestic showers and washdown facilities run off, and was not a sealed system but does have external access points. This was the most logical entry point as the water was treated as non-human waste and was a system that did not interface with the sewage treatment plant directly.

Darlene remained unsure and glanced over the blueprints of the base. 'Erica, are you sure you are not a plumber.' Then smirked. 'Listen you guys, here at the Eastern end of the facility there is a large generator plant and that is the powerhouse that run base the systems, I think we want to avoid that location at all costs. Now if we enter this gate here, the one marked - Delta 1/2, it looks like we can reach the medical building underground which is just three hundred metres away in a westerly direction. From there on we could potentially find uniforms and other shit for disguise.' Erica then nodded along with Hastings, then commented. 'Right so once we get to DARPA we can be dropped off a kilometre or so away from the main complex then find this inlet or outlet housing thing at Delta whatever.

That all seems pretty straight forward.' Erica then asked a question. 'And how do we ensure that we can fight these Claw creatures off if we meet them?' Hastings rubbed his hands together and answered. 'In reality, we do not, our priority is to get the heavy armoured gates open into the science labs if we can overcome the military guards, then let the hybrid beasties do the rest, TA and the Igigi will be waiting nearby or should be, but I certainly wish that An'Mer was with us. By now he will be on his way striking at the Mars complex with An'Gregaar and the Anunnaki with the Hive crews. So, I think firstly, let us get to the Whitehouse and see how we can disrupt the communications to the Claw from there.'

As the girls gathered together what belongings they had, TA had re-entered the chamber. 'I have heard that the 'beasts' have been moved to the Nevada plains, it appears that they are quite an aggressive breed and may be difficult to control. I am not sure that we should let these unbridled apex predators loose on the ground unless we are well away from them.' Erica smirked. 'Well, if we don't let them do their thing then the Claw will continue to murder mankind which to say the least who en-masse are quite the innocent party in this universal charade. I think I recall that we are the actual **'alien'** breed and the children of the stars on this planet, or the new world prodigy or even the modern equivalent to a **test tube slave society** that seems to be part of this game that we are playing.'

TA then answered. 'The Claw are the evil that begets evil, trust me folks this is not about nurturing or the betterment of humankind, this is about their actual termination and extermination by galactic vermin that has some great issue with their own creators and, I have no idea about the real why? Perhaps they want to really eradicate the humankind on earth and keep the whole planet for themselves as they cannot seem to reconcile their differences with the Anunnaki.'

Erica jumped straight into the conversation with her own ideas. 'So as far as I am concerned once we identify where these Claw creatures are hanging out, we should release the hybrid 'beasts' to go and strike without question but, before we do, please tell me something mister TA?

How did you actually transport the beasts to Nevada from the laboratories after their re-capture?' TA smiled. 'Oh! my dear lady that part was easy, we simply put them to sleep and loaded them into the Pleidian craft then they were dumped into the **tanker trucks** and then the Pleiadeans did the rest. You know the vehicles that Hastings called the fish tanks.'

Darlene then smirked and muttered. 'What was the chances that we should have actually ended up in those tanks with flipper and free willy, let alone a few deranged apex killers to boot, and we could have quite literally ended up being dead meat by now.' TA squeezed a smile. Erica was also smirking. 'Yep, plan B, get in through the piping for sure.'

Chapter Twenty – Seven:

'Talking with God'

It was not long before the Pleiadian transport craft had arrived at the temple of Hathor and Kemp and the girls had entered the craft quietly as it hovered just a few feet off the ground and out of sight of the main thoroughfare. This was the location where most of the visitors would normally have congregated for their tours. Hastings had spoken with TA and they agreed that they needed a way to remove the contact tower or Obelisk at the American Mall park near the Whitehouse in Washington, and decided that physically blowing the monument up was not going to be the ideal solution, and they had to think of something less devasting but effective.

As the crew were silently jetting towards the USA, Erica leaned forward in the cockpit and offered a suggestion. 'Kemp, we don't really have to destroy it, do we? We just need to confuse it, after all it's only a techy radio tower.' Darlene began nodding her head in agreement then offered her own unorthodox way of dealing with such technical problems and from her mindset this normally included the use of a fourteen-pound mash hammer and an Army full of brute force and ignorant soldiers to wield it, suffice to say that subtlety was not Darlene's strongest subject, then she commented further.

'Yes of course Erica we can send a huge god killing electromagnetic or radioactive pulse down through the Whitehouse dining room, out of the front door, then down the lawn and over the water basin then drive it down Pennsylvania Avenue and right into the Mall park and hit the big nasty tower smack on, voila! one confused Obelisk! Erica stared at Hastings and then back at Darlene in almost disbelief and smiled politely. Then she pointed her pointy finger at Hastings and retorted in kind. 'Well, Darlene perfect, sounds like a solid theory and should do the trick, but I don't think so, but, I bet you that Kemp has a solution already lurking in that pea of human and Anunnaki thinking grey cell, he calls his brain?'

Hastings laughed out loudly at them both and then presented his thoughts. 'Well, actually ladies I think I do have a solution, I would just crash a big jetliner aeroplane into it and bring the whole thing toppling down, that would work of sure, but firstly because I cannot really fly an aeroplane and secondly I don't have an aeroplane, I think that option would be a bit of a challenge for me, but, in reality what we do have at our disposal girls is a Pleiadian transport shuttle craft that emits huge streams of electromagnetic energy, and Darlene, by default you have just solved our wee problem, thank you.

All we need to do is get the Pleiadian pilot to rest this craft on top of the apex or as near as we can over the Ben Ben capstone and power up a few thousand zillion, gazillion of gigawatz from the propulsion power-train and concentrate its energy on the tower and zaaap! We overload the complete kit and keboodle, I think that should do the trick.'

Erica was thinking deeply and wondering about all the miniscule snip bits of information they were missing. She was thinking that it was a very novel idea indeed, and in the minds of lesser intellectual individuals it would be almost unfathomable to work out. But she would have quite happily dismissed the concept as perhaps far too radical.

But, for Hastings it was his intellect that kept him sparking. Although the Pleiadian craft was a **drone operated** machine and not really piloted by a living being who could respond and obviously cannot speak the common language of English. Erica then passed further comment. 'You are going to have to explain that idea to the pilot droid Kemp.' Then he responded swifty.

'I know Erica don't worry I am working on it.' He then removed a pen and a small piece of paper from his pocket, and, whilst taking his artistry to another level completely, he drew a rough picture of the Pleiadian craft sitting over top of the obelisk. Although it was not quite a Picasso or a Lautrec in any slap dash mastery presentation, but to Hastings it was no different to any ancient hieroglyph or cave marking or drawing he had seen in his many travels. He then presented his masterpiece to the synthetic droid that remained ostensibly void of all contact and any emotion. When, as if on cue the head of the droid suddenly spun around on its axis and the four cameras with their blue concentrated tiny circling neon lights zoomed in on the drawing. And then concentrated its AI lens directly at Hastings in what may well become the first true digital WTF AI response of disbelief moment in technical history. Then a yellow light was illuminated on the screen panel across the front flight console, it was a full display of the Hastings not so highly technical drawing that was emerging on what looked like a three dimensional computer screen with small energy pulses or light sources being flashed digitally across the screen.

It was then that the craft performed a three-hundred and sixty degree spin on its own axis, and then shot off at a great rate of knots. And within a split nanusecond the crew found themselves heading towards the home of the United States President of America and had arrived in Washington within eleven minutes.

The president of the country who at this juncture in time was certainly out to lunch. But the military radar and defence systems were already on high alert. And by default, it was not long thereafter, that two hundred and twelve thousand three hundred and seven UFO sightings were being reported to the state emergency services. Which quickly jammed the news networks switchboards via the mass media coverage across the country.

Each person having reported that an alien craft had been seen hovering over the Whitehouse and was now apparently resting over the top of the great homemade built Obelisk. The Pleiadian droid pilot had done its task and the communications link between the USA based Igigi and Draco would certainly be disrupted for at least another few hours.

- *(Apparently in NASA terms of investigation with extreme data analyisis review undertaken by their top boffins which was deemed more than a sufficient amount of time to write a full-scale investigative report of at least 220 pages about explaining to the masses why yet another failed weather balloon was being flown across the capital).*

The craft then left the Washington area and was directed to Baalbek in Lebanon where the Draco were to be engaged.

Chapter Twenty – Eight:

'Sushi Patrol'

The Igigi assault party had landed at Nevada springs Groom lake, when TA had brought the convoy of two trucks near to the one kilometre border exclusion area at the intersection of D1 and D2, then halted. The security perimeter gate was clearly signposted by a large yellow notice board that stated:

- **D1/D2 WARNING: this area is a military controlled zone that may or may not TEST MILITARY weapons or DANGEROUS chemicals that could injure, maim or kill animals or life stock that venture into or/are permitted to enter this zone without authorization. YOU have been warned. USA Home Guard.**

TA then simply ignored the placard and pulled out a small hand tool from his pocket and pointed it at the industrial padlock and heavy steel chain, then waited.

Within twenty seconds the locking device had melted and fallen to the sandy floor below. He then noticed a green vapour trail of an incoming object in the sky and followed its flight path with great interest as it jolted from left to right in the night sky then appeared to have touched down somewhere within the DARPA complex near to the stations power house. He knew that it was not Kemp and the girls in the Pleiadian craft as they were tripping the light fantastic in the United States and Lebanon, although he also knew that it could not be An'Mer or the Merlithian team either, as they were already Mars bound.

Was this Shamgaz the Claw leader? And had he somehow managed to secure a Draco craft having been supposedly wandering within the vast Nevada desert wreaking havoc in his wake. Or after killing the base commander he had never actually left the complex at all but had sent another rogue Claw beast into the wilderness as a deliberate distraction, thus, taking attention away from DARPA installation. Which in reality meant that a hybrid beast could still be at large and potentially nearby. TA turned his attention toward the Igigi crew that had joined him and explained the plan in a bit more detail. They were simply going to have to wait until they acknowledged that the Pleiadian craft with Hastings and the girls on bord had landed safely at the Delta boundary gates, before they would attempt to deliver their food stock to the camp in anticipation whilst hoping to gain entrance.

He explained to the loyal Igigi that they would wait until being contacted by Hastings first before making any further moves. But had no idea what the actual signal was going to be. The TA team had waited patiently since ambushing and hijacking the trucks earlier, and they knew they would have to enter the camp before dusk or before 18:25 hours as that was when the military security guards would change out their security duties. And certainly, before any suspicions could be raised about a late arrival at the base as the military would be expecting the delivery on time. TA and the team had acquired both boiler suits and ID badges for their part of the mission and rehearsed how they would approach the military base.

Meanwhile, the Pleiadian Pilot Droid had landed at Baalbek in the Lebanon un-noticed and had set the craft down plumb on a colossal standing granite platform in front of the great Baachus temple and then waited patiently.

Hastings and the girls exited the craft and stealthily approached the old grand temple, luckily there was no one around to witness their arrival thank goodness, and there was no spectators. And then the team began searching for the Baalbek keystone which would be easily identifiable by a large Ankh and snake carving enshrouded within an old Sumerian-styled oval cartouche. But, first they would have to locate the Western wall and the blocked up entrance that resembled a monolith, not unlike a Stonehenge feature in design. Which from their brief understanding from TA that it should be located at an apex corner of two boundary walls.

The chamber itself was the ancient communications complex that served the Anunnaki for local command and control of their ancient craft. After several minutes had passed by, Darlene had walked along the giant stone plinths that led to the corner of the crumbled building and gazed over the complete complex from her vantage point. 'Wow! Look at these things they are huge, these blocks must be at least be 100 tons in weight if not more.' She remarked. Erica then took a few seconds and also gazed over the grand massive structure and responded. 'Darlene these plinths are at least 500 or even 1000 tons each and look at this amazing almost unbelievable engineering. They are all aligned and very flat. This must have been an important place in its day, can you feel the vibrations and heat from these stones.'

Hastings had caught up with the girls and asked for any clues. 'Any luck ladies, I cannot get the unbelievable size and design of this place, and look my bracelet it is going haywire, I think we must be near an energy source.' Darlene stepped around the corner and identified what she thought could only be the hidden doorway and acknowledged the huge lintel that sat above the granite door frame was at least ten foot in height and probably weighed a couple of tons then she spied the entrance way itself. 'I think I have found it, here look it's the same as you and TA described Kemp.'

Hastings made a fist with his left hand then let out an excited squeal. 'Yes, and very well spotted indeed, Darlene.' He said in an almost condescending childish manner. Darlene just smiled back at him. He then started fumbling about in his robes and produced the golden Ankh relic that was normally attached to the top of his staff given to him by the Anunnaki at Ahgartha. Then noticed that his arm bracelet had stopped rotating but was now glowing and vibrating. He reached out his left arm to make contact with the stonework, and the bracelet begun to rotate slowly in an anti-clockwise direction not unlike a magnetic compass and then he very nonchalantly he placed the Ankh into the recess of the upright plinth.

'Look it fits perfectly.' After a couple of seconds the Ankh began to display a soft blue glow of light then Hastings froze in his sandals and appeared to be bolt upright as a yellow glow had also started to form around the cartouche on the plinth, Hastings simultaneously had almost lit up like a human Christmas tree light. Both Erica and Darlene stepped back several paces simultaneously just in case it was going to start sparking, and then watched in wonderment as his body became consumed in the intense glow under his robes.

'What in the name of hell's half acre is happening to you Kemp?' Exclaimed Erica! and moved a little closer. 'Hastings then spoke out in a very soft but commanding tone. 'It is okay ladies, just stay where you are, I think, I am making a phone call! I am also wearing an Anunnaki shakra vibration mantle that An'Mer gave me to wear, it apparently tunes into several frequencies in the Anunnaki communications matrix like a radio transmitter and, he says, if you think hard enough about what you want or who you want to connect with, then somehow it works.

But I cannot seem to connect to whoever is listening.' Darlene started clicking her fingers together. 'Yes, we know Kemp, we have them as well, An'Laara had passed them on to us.' Erica then commented. 'The Anunnaki are certainly aware that we are all here together and that we must engage with the Draco, and make some sort of contact with them or Shamgaz, as Lilith had stipulated very clearly.

To me it makes no sense at all whatsoever what her rationale for doing this actually is, so please don't ask me how it really works either as I have not a clue.' Hastings was becoming quite numb and was staring directly at the wall as Darlene conversed with Erica.

'The Anunnaki must have calibrated this **stone** tablet to direct its energy from this location and maybe towards the base at DARPA, and my thinking is that they can pinpoint Shamgaz's location or his command centre. But most likely my guess is that they can target the Axumite star keys. That is why we had to knockout the Obelisk at Washington and shut down certain communications chains.'

As Hastings waited patiently in his numbed state of mind there was a sensation of heat tingling that was running up and down the middle of his spine and he leaned over to one side as if he was in discomfort. He then reached out and placed his other hand on the stone doorway and bowed his head as if he was about to pray. There was a moment of dizziness and nausea erupting within his head then he heard the distant chorus of multiple voices or a distant echoing that had started to hum around in his mind, he could not make any sense of the first few million murmurs, then 'pop' as clear as day a single voice broke his concentration. It was a tone that he did not recognise, but it all sounded, rough and almost gargled in its delivery. After a few seconds or more the background noise had died away and then recognisable speech hit his earshot, he could make out what he thought was being said.

'We are waiting here for our weapons, where are the remaining Claw they should be here by now, this is Shamgaz, where are my soldiers and what are the Anunnaki up to?'

The tone was almost as if the speaker was slurring his words combined with a touch of drunkenness and anger albeit, he heard the odd hiss and splurgle of mixed tones as the Claw commander spoke, but he did not recognise anything else. As time slowly passed by everything around him had become a complete blur and the space around him seemed to have slowed down to a snail's arse pace, it was then that he took a very deep breath then responded to the Draco directly.

'The Dominion are not going to bow down to your ludicrous demands Shamgaz, taking control of the human military and the attack on Mars will only give you moments if not seconds longer to exist on this planet and across dimension. You of all species know and understand the Anunnaki will take

revenge not only on you, but your home planet as well, and millions will suffer because of your inane actions. You have failed in your miserable attempts to overthrow the human construct and bring the Anunnaki legacy to an end. Shamgaz, your days on this planet and this plain are numbered. The stench of your toxic serpentine legacy will come to a very abrupt sticky end if you decide to continue in this madcap endeavour. If you do not give up on this assault of yours now, or you shall face the powers of the great Pantheon Triad, the choice is yours. Or, be gone with you. The Anunnaki and the council will give you one cycle of the Mars's moon to decide.'

Shamgaz's skin tightened up on hearing the one voice that he hated so much. And his own lizard skin felt like it was crawling all over with tiny cold irritating beasties scurrying around under the layer of his protective scales. The astral angel of death and the underworld Queen of ethereal demise had crawled into his life and so un-announced.

This was the haunting tones of the **'Lilith'** albeit, in her physical presence and ultra-dominating stature. Any attack he planned was going to be fought till the death, but, this was the one entity that any alien entity feared the most. These trans-dimensional shape shifters such as Lilith (Inanna) do have the powers to deal with the Draco rather swiftly. But on the earths playfield it was a different ball game entirely and had a multitude of cosmic rules to follow in any face to face contact but, Shamgaz had no idea that 'Lilith' was even awake and that many years ago Hastings and the humans had inadvertently disturbed her slumber. But the cosmos works in many weird and wonderous ways and the wakening of an Anunnaki body was going to be part of the process. Shamgaz risked all then shouted out.

'You don not frighten me with your ancient war cries Lilith, or whatever name you call yourself these days, I am here to take revenge for the Claw on behalf of our Cobra Queen who now dwells as our ruler within the Minerva belt. And my Queen wants revenge for killing the Draaken King.

Lilith retorted with an eloquent response.

'Aaah! Shamgaz, it is you! I remember that particular event so very well as if it was only yesterday as we stood by and watched a mere human take down your almighty great king warrior in the most undignified of manners, very slap dash Shamgaz. But be informed that we also permitted the animal kingdom to devour his inert carcass and we watched on with great amusement as the beasts munched away at his torn limbs, until all was consumed. He was a worthless leader and certainly no match for the Anunnaki, and I am glad to state that you are no better either.'

It was then that another voice broke the silence.

'Shamgaz, bow down on your serpentine skull and pray homage to the great Hathor and to the house of Horus, your ancient ways have re-surfaced, and yet you think that you can hold the great Pantheon collective to any sort of ransom. We await your sorry carcass to be delivered to our domain in seven blood-stained pieces, and each segment will be a gift to the great seven judges and overlords.'

Then Hastings simply stopped speaking. Darlene and Erica stood open mouthed almost in awe and waited to see what happened next. Hastings then clenched his fists together again and broke contact with the stone and relaxed as if nothing had actually happened. Erica stepped forward and grabbed him by the arm and removed the Ankh icon slowly from the cartouche and passed comment. 'Kemp are you alright, Kemp can you hear me, its us Darlene and Erica.' She asked with a real concern in her voice regarding his current state of mind. She was silently praying that the event had not fried his pea sized Anunnaki brain cell to a crisp.

Hastings looked at them both in a haze and bewilderment and just smiled. 'Damnation, nothing, I could not make any contact at all, zada, zilch, zero, I just have this weird buzzing and crackling in my ears.' Darlene then placed a hand on his brow and looked into eyes. 'Well, let me tell you, I have seen some really strange shit in my time Kemp, but your face literary transformed into another face entirely, I did not recognise it, and your voice, well it was that of two women. Did'nt know you were an astral ventriloquist either.' The Imperial protector ran his hand through his hair. 'What do you mean ventriloquist?'

Darlene responded. 'We both heard it clear as day, did'nt we Erica, but tell us something? Whywould you say such a thing as a threat to antagonise this Shamgaz? he is going to go absolutely bananas.' Erica clasped her hands together then offered her point of view. 'It was Lilith's voice we heard Darlene, well the first one was, that one was for sure, as I keep hearing the same name Lilith right this very minute ringing in my head and it is still repeating over and over. Maybe, this is why? we came here to ensure that the location at Ahgartha was not compromised and the Anunnaki might be able to determine that Shamgaz is actually on the planet and accruing his troops.

And that he must have a craft with communications or has the Axum tablets with him. I think we need to go quickly folks.' The three agreed then returned to their waiting craft. 'Where are we off to now.' Asked Darlene with a hint of excitement in her voice as they walked back along the huge granite blocks towards the waiting craft. Hastings looked up at the stars. 'I think it is time

'The Seed': 'Anu – Nexus'

to get to DARPA and shut down this Shamgaz for once and for all time.' Erica then removed her backpack and checked the zipper.

'Well, Kemp we only heard half of that conversation from you, and we never heard anything else that was spoken by others to you. Can you remember anything at all?' He nodded to the effect that his brain cell was set on 'Delete mode', and his memory was blank. Erica then clutched at her back-pack. 'Well, no worries, I have another very unpleasant surprise for mister Shamgaz, I hope he likes gardening as I have a brew that he is not going to take too kindly to.' Hastings grinned a huge grin.

'Did you make up that plant concoction after all Erica.' She winked back at him. 'Yep, but there is a little extra compound I have added for good measure, a dash of sulphuric acid. The same mix that certainly took care of the lizard infestation in the atrium. Your idea of a test was quite enlightening.' Darlene was almost impressed. 'My goodness Erica your little green fingers are becoming quite a deadly touch, we will have to call you lady hemlock from now on.' She nodded her head in response. 'Could be.'

Meanwhile, at the military Listening post at SETI Berkeley in the United States the **'Listen'** project communications centre or to give the base its nickname of ET Central was buzzing with a hive of activity as the top end computers began streaming and churning out large reams of binary print data and numbers that had been recorded, and the 'alien' transmission was as clear as a bright summers day to any mathematics gurus or teachers. But, for us mere mortals it was as clear as the Serengeti watering hole mud.

Doctor Brendan Hinkelman the project commander was in a fit of almost exultation and excitement as he suddenly grabbed a fistful of the data sheets and ran the complete length of the communications office complex and corridors in an effort to find his military superior and report or even try to explain what had just occurred. It was during this short time that SETI was supposedly shut down temporarily and the top-secret security chiefs had dismissed all non-essential personnel from the listening post, whilst the Pentagon ordered a DEFCON One Red alert status across all military and nuclear installations, just as four strike F15 and three F16 aircraft and three stealth aircraft had taken to the skies. NATO was certainly taking the transmission as a super 'WOW' moment.

Chapter Twenty - Nine:

'Warning'

As the Ethiopian Clerics sat huddled around large oak table in the church vestry a single technician had entered the room and had engaged with the group. 'Gentlemen I am sorry to trouble you during this most important meeting, but I have just been viewing the drone footage again and found something rather odd and perhaps exciting. I was playing with the colour definitions on the monitor to get a clearer view, when I noticed that sitting under the mercy seat lid at the top of the 'tabot' I could make out some writings. It looks to me like it is written in latin or other language and this image remained there for just a few seconds, but we have it recorded. It is only visible through ultra-violet light.' The chief cleric leaned over and quizzed the screen, sure enough there was several lines of writing and he traced the lettering with his forefinger, then started to read out the words to his peer group. 'My latino linguisti is not so perfect but these appear to be an early Deunos script text..' He said almost jokingly as he tried to decipher the message from the Gods.

'It reads that there is a war coming from an **ancient time in Sumeria**, and appears to be recorded by **Thoth.'** He then gazed at the assembly. 'I think it says:

1. There will be **poison** in the waters for **Kings and Queens who consume the gold** of the Pharaohs, I presume this is some kind of warning.
2. The woman **Lilith who takes the seed of man by force**. I should think by deception or whilst man slumbers and perhaps the antagonist as this Lilith is a historical dangerous underworld entity.
3. The **Anunnaki say there is no medicine against the power of death** - I interpret this as a great war is imminent and no survivors will remain.
4. Delivered by the snake in the grass by the **Snake People who state if they cannot gain entry into heaven then, they will raise hell,** on earth and I think this may be alluding to this war somewhere?

- **Hoc est bellum:** *This is war*
- **Ab antique:** *Sumeria in ancient times*
- **Ab origine:** *from the source 'Thoth'*
- **Aqua fortis:** *a toxic acid Nitric Acid to dissolve all but gold and platinum*
- **Bella Mullier qui hominum allicit et accipit eos per fortis:** *Lilith – women who lure men and takes them by force.*
- *Anunnaki*

  contra vim mortis non crescit herba (or salvia) in hortis – There is no medicine against the power of Death.
- **Serpentis hominid:** Snake people
- **ophidio in herba** hidden in the grass
- **Lectere si nequeo superos Acheronta movebo** – If we cannot reach heaven we will raise hell.
- **The third planet from the sun.**

'Well gentlemen that seems to be all I can make of this strange message, we know there was no forced entry into the shrine and the underground passage has been sealed for centuries now. So we can eliminate any secret or clandestine play at work, therefore, we may have to assume that the **space people** have returned to earth and reclaimed their iconic property. And perhaps use our relics for a more clandestine purpose.

Maybe this icon is part of the solution to deal with this war in the stars or here on earth that this writing depicts the prophecy of war alluded to so often? I should think that if this is part of the legacy of the Ark is by design then these outside visitors are indeed our holy God figures. We must be very careful who we talk to and what we say to the external community.'

Chapter Thirty:

'Assault'

The Pleiadian craft had settled down on the soft sand silently, then the occupants gathered their belongings together and made their way to the entrance gates at zone D1/D2. Within seconds after touch-down the Pleiadian craft was already heaven bound without a whisper or indication of its swift departure. Darlene was first to pass through the security gates and took a three sixty view of the area before she spoke.

'Looks like the gates are already open Kemp, a bit odd for a high security military installation, maybe TA and the Igigi have been here already?' Hastings scoured the local area, then casually bent down onto one knee and picked up a piece of the heavy chain that lay embedded in the sand and passed his response. 'Yep, most definitely looks like it, and we are not alone Darlene because this chain has been melted as opposed to being ripped apart by the use of a 'Crowe bar'. The group then scattered around the sand mounds with the intention of seeking the entrance to the D1 pipework, and quite quickly found the concrete blocks and protection cage that led the aquatic way into the water treatment systems. As they wrestled with the large metal gates to enter the drain, Erica caught a glimpse of two Chinook heavy lift helicopters which had appeared in her view and were sitting on the nearby runway, both girls observed several 'un' human like figures stepping one by one out of the choppers and onto the black basalt apron of the base. 'Get down! Cried Erica very sternly.

'It looks to me like the Draco have some new recruits but look at how these uniformed soldiers are moving around, they are not articulated as we are, it looks like their limbs have been filled up with a bucket of nuts and bolts.' Hastings took a few more seconds and observed the arrivals. Judging by the movement and the type of species then contemplated as to what he thought he was looking at, they were certainly not human. Then made a very flippant remark.

'The Seed': 'Anu – Nexus'

'Yikes, girls we have two things going on here. One, those soldiers are defo micro chipped in some way or other and may as well sing 'tik tok' as they march along. Two, the other ones the arrivals, I am not so sure, they might be our problem. They could be the Draco reinforcements for sure and what I think is that they are another species entirely. They look very thin for a cannibalistic lizard. I have counted twelve in all, but they will be stronger than us, better keep your anti snake poison bottle handy Erica, we will probably need it, and we had better be careful.'

The three then entered the tunnel and slowly made their way through the underground concrete jungle and the well-designed waters system. Within three minutes they soon came to a junction point where two equally sized tunnels merged together. Darlene reached into her satchel and retrieved her trusty handlamp, Erica meanwhile, had grabbed her bottle of snake and lizard repellent and was at the ready to spray any unwelcome lizardy snakey type beasties that they may encounter en-route.

Kemp stared back at them both and smirked. 'Well, Darlene, you are quite the Doctor Livingstone of this journey, which way now?' He asked. Darlene pulled out a sketch that she had made earlier and suggested the left tunnel as it looked cleaner with less water on the floor and pointed the flashlight deep into the tunnel.

In doing so there was a hint of a flash back from the other end which could denote a hatchway. Kemp then led the group to the other end whilst avoiding the odd rat that had skirmished by. Eventually they reached an exit point or a solid concrete wall, which had a single fixed steel ladder attached that reached up the wall face only a few feet and stopped short of a swing type heavy steel panel. The stencilled sign on the facia read: '**Service hatch D1**. He ascended the ladder and took a quick peek through the thin metal mesh and sure enough he could identify what he thought was a modern medical facility.

He then whispered to the girls. 'Well done indeed Darlene, you are spot on, we are at the medical post, I cannot see or hear any movement inside.' He then grappled with the metal swing gate and eventually managed to pull down the tee shaped handle an opened the plate that was mounted on the two large hinges attached to one side of the bulkhead, almost losing his footing in the process as the plate broke free, then unexpectedly it sprang inwards. After assuring himself that that the proverbial coast was clear inside the room he slid on his belly through the hatch and into the ultra-clean clinic, then assisted the girls into the treatment cubicle. Erica stood upright and wiped herself down.

'That was not so bad.' She said softly. 'Much better than using the alternative aquatic option.' Then grabbed at Darlene's jacket and assisted her entry into the lab. Kemp had found a pair of white coveralls hanging on the hooks behind the door and handed them out to the girls. 'Here, these should do the trick.' The clinic was medically very well equipped with surgical instruments strewn everywhere, and a range of electronic microscopes that sat upright like three soldiers standing on parade ready for inspection, and what looked like an incubator chamber with a couple of microwave ovens that were set out across a stainless-steel bench. He grabbed a fistful of large syringes from the yellow Tupperware container and motioned Erica to fill them up with her snake 'luvvin' toxin. Whilst simultaneously taking a glimpse through the metal window blinds where he spied several uniformed soldiers standing at the main gate about a hundred metres or so away. But oddly enough they were not exactly doing soldiery type of activity, they were almost moving in synchronicity and appeared to be escorted by a smaller figure who managed their every movement via a handheld device.

'I think this whole complex has been taken over.' He muttered then concentrated his attention towards the main headquarters building and watched as the new arrivals were being systematically led one by one into the basement of the office block. It was then that a feint rattling sound could be heard within one of the clinic office cupboards behind them and the whole team froze instantly and remained very quiet. Hastings picked up a large clay pestle and intended to strike first and forget any questions until later and simultaneously grabbed the handle of the wooden door and quickly yanked it open ready to strike. To his amazement he was confronted by a young man who was writhing down on the floor below him in cold fear and huddled into one corner.

Darlene instinctively had raised her syringe and was ready to pounce and inject her first victim. 'Stop! Hastings cried out then placed his hand on the syringe. 'Do not be too hasty Darlene.' Then on bended knees he reached forward into the closet and opened his hands up, and spoke in a very controlled tone.

'Calm down, no need to panic, we are here to help.' He raised his hand up to his mouth and muttered. 'Shhh, we need your help. We need to open the main gate.' The young man started nodding his head in acknowledgement then spoke very softly. 'I am Seth one of the new medical interns, I am a biology student, I have only been here a few days when all this shit hit the fan, and I have been hiding in here ever since. There are aliens in this place and they have taken over the compound. Those creature things have also murdered several of my colleagues and taken control of the bio-labs over there in the big blue building. For some reason they don't come near here, I think it is because of the radiation levels in this unit are high or it could be the nearby sewage waste disposal unit. I think it is the smell that is keeping them away.' Erica then joined in the conversation. 'Do you know how to open the gates Seth? We have to let some very important transport trucks into the base.' The young student nodded his head as an indication of yes. Then answered very hesitantly. 'The guards are all drones, I have watched them for ages, they don't actually do very much, but basically wait and watch the main building. And carry a hand-held torch thing that seems to act as a communicator.

But only the two taller officers have them.' Erica breathed a deep sigh and then asked another barrage of questions. 'Seth, do you have any military uniforms here? and do you think you could get near to the main gate and act like one of them soldiers?' The intern then pointed to the next office. 'Doctor Zeiss has a Major's uniform in his office, it is through there, second door on the right, but I am afraid he his dead. His uniform is too large for me to wear, but it would probably fit you.' He said pointing to Hastings.

Both Erica and Darlene stared at Hastings and expectant of a response. 'Okay, but I will need a wee distraction from you guys to allow me to get close enough and enter into the guard post. And I will need a shave.' Erica, smiled. 'No worries we will think of something, you go get dressed.'

After several minutes the new cleanly shaved **Major Kemp Hastings** appeared back in the clinic and presented his new Army attire to the girls. 'Does this look okay. He asked. 'Will I pass any alien scrutiny?' Darlene was first to respond. 'Looks great, I would probably date you myself, if did not know you any better.' She then leaned forward and removed the name tag from his jacket. 'No loose ends.' She said. The young intern then stood upright and had almost composed himself back to normality then passed comment.

'The aliens will leave shortly, and the guards will go into the mess hall to eat soon. This normally happens as soon as the big spotlights come on. The aliens do not seem to like any light. The inner gate is only manned by one man and a second person sits at the control console in the guardhouse. That is where the barrier controls are housed, nothing manual in this place, I am afraid.'

Hastings then tucked his shirt into the back of his trousers and asked another question. 'So, there are two gates into this compound?' The intern pointed out of the window toward the entrance gates. 'There is an inner gate and an outer gate, look, here, you can see the narrow corridor in between the two. The outer gate is a simple mechanical gate but the inner gate leading here into the test complex is an electronic one.'

Hastings checked his pockets and then proceeded to leave the building via the front door hoping to raise no suspicions as he walked in robot fashion towards the gatehouse and started muttering to himself. 'This had better work out or we are going to be sushi by morning.' And kept mumbling away to himself as he 'tick tocked' his way towards the gate house. On reaching the front steps to the guard room he stared directly at the on - station guard at the barrier for a few seconds then marched right on into the control room without any challenge or confrontation and found the gate operator sitting at his desk. The soldier was just staring out the window into nothingness without a care in the world. 'Everything all right soldier.' He asked, then waited for a response. The trooper stood upright and in soldier like fashion he saluted in response with the wrong hand and then instantly sat down again. Hastings did not flinch an inch. He then slowly walked towards the back of the room and waited for a few seconds, thinking as to how he was going to distract the guard from his staring out of the window duties.

Just then, there was an almighty crash! of thunder in the background as the bulk of a thirty foot long, twenty-ton tanker full of gods great aquatic creatures struck the forward metal gates at sixty miles an hour sending mud, shit and strips of long stainless-steel and wire mesh everywhere, puffs of soft brown sand formed an array of clouds as the heavy-duty Michelin tyres ripped through the dusty trackway. The vehicle continued through to the second set of barriers ripping the steel posts out of the ground like toothpicks as the monster machine juggernaut cascaded along out of control and effectively knocked down the so-called heavy steel forged security gates. Everything around him seemed to slow down again and Hastings could not believe what he was witnessing. The delivery truck eventually stopped somewhere in the middle of the compound.

When things had eventually settled down, a number of staff appeared in the central parade square and pretty much did nothing, then Hastings spied TA sliding out the cab of the truck and was making his way towards the medical clinic building. There was moment when Hastings spied one of the visitors in the crowd of six clad in an apron and was wielding what looked like a butcher's cleaver and a hacksaw that were certainly covered in blood. But not blood from the occupants of the truck but from whatever was on the evening menu in the cellar of the headquarters building.

'Shit, I hope they are having a barbecue with bacon, beef and potatoes, and not the leg of the commanding officer's driver served with cheese and cauliflower sauce.' He smirked. Just then a second truck appeared through the damaged entrance and quite literally ripped through the wire mesh fencing missing the gate completely, it then cascaded across the walkway and struck the central flag post then collided with the wingtip of a phantom four alpha aircraft that was the centre piece of DARPA's Annex C test facility entrance, and pretty much acted as a technical welcome to the station.

But the impact of the collision had ripped the port side wing off the jet completely and spun the airframe around, one hundred and eighty degree on its axis. Hastings instinctively ran from the guard room and was soon confronted by the external guard who was both covered in dust and staring back at him.

The soldier stood his ground and remained quite motionless. He watched on as the soldier's eyes seem to be struggling to focus on him, and then he spoke. 'I am private first class, Samuel Heavensent and I am from Nevada. Where are you from?' The soldier asked. And as if on demand TA had struck the soldier from behind with a rather large red fire extinguisher that he had retrieved from the fire point, then spoke. 'Hastings that tanker over there is going to blow up at any moment and the beasties and the fish have already escaped. We need to find safety from the Draco lair before their reinforcements arrive. Where are your princesses?

Tell me what have do done with those angels?' Hastings gazed across the station at the carnage left by the timely arrival of the fish tankers then at the HQ building. 'The girls are safe, I thought you were going to wait for my signal before you entered the base?' TA laughed out loudly on hearing his remarks. 'Well, I would have waited as we agreed, but the Igigi people saw the Draco craft arrive and had been spooked. After which they decided they had done too much waiting and took matters into their own hands. Do not be too surprised as this is what you get when you deal with little green men.'

Hastings was smirking then motioned TA to follow him back across the open square towards the medical centre where to their surprise found that Darlene and Erica had been locked in the office of the ex- Doctor Zeiss, as he could see they were peering through the little square window in the door back at them. But, sadly they also found the lifeless body of the young bio-intern lying on the floor outside the bio lab, appearing to have been sliced almost in two by a rather large scalpel. Hastings unlocked the door to the office and let the girls out. 'Hey Erica, Darlene how are you two, what happened here?' Erica raised her hand up to her mouth and pointed to the adjacent office.

'One of those things is in there.' She said softly. Then held up the large plastic spray bottle. Hastings grabbed her attention. 'Get it straight in the eyes or in its throat, and don't miss, that should do the trick. Have you both got your syringes? I think you had better give a couple to TA as well.' Hastings took the bottle from Erica and gave it a squirt into the air, then glared back at Erica.

'Remind me never to piss you off at any time in the future, I would hate to think what nasty's you would have in store for me in order inflict great pain apart from your cooking of course.' Erica's face said it all and he knew when to shut up and just go to work.

His work being having to deal with an imminent attack from a young super strong lizard entity from another planet that was busy testing the medical inventory in building 'C'. To Hastings it sounded as if world-war three was being enacted and the office equipment was being tested for tensile strength and robust **bangability** judging by the sounds of the steel trays and bowls being thrust against the walls and windows, along with each drawer having being pulled out of their cabinets and strewn across the floor.

'I wonder what it is looking for?' He whispered. Then took a very deep breath and slowly opened the door to the office as the huge creature was about to throw the desktop computer and screen at the far wall. Hastings then tried to break the proverbial ice.

'Do you know the cost of those computer things, and they are so very difficult to reboot, and let me tell you, if you forget or loss your password, then that's when you are in really deep 'pooh' just like you are going to be very soon.'

The lizard figure stood in almost disbelief as it contemplated not only the presence of Hastings, but the fact that he appeared and not to be too displaced by its awesome presence and perhaps deemed this as an insult. Then, the beast lunged forward at him whilst reaching out and grabbing him by his newly ironed military uniform and picked him straight up off the floor and in one dismissive thrust threw him against the far bulkhead. The impact had certainly shaken him but he was aware his shakra belt was protecting him. He then tried to intimidate the beast just a little more.

'So, you do not want to play ball at all do you.' He answered then pulled out the syringe as the beast came closer for a second time. But, in doing so, Hastings suffered a very sharp striking pain in his spine then thrust his arm out and grabbed the Lizard by the throat and rammed the syringe directly into its neck vein and squeezed the plunger until the instrument was near empty. The animal instantly let him drop to the floor and grappled at its own throat and was clearly struggling to open its own airway as the toxic plant juices did their nasty horrible job and started to break down the animal's natural bodily defences.

But unfortunately for this **alien Ghecko creature**, it was too late. Hastings and the girls stood by the doorway and watched as the remaining skin tissue of the Claw started to go through a transformational natural skin (shedding) change not unlike a normal snake. Albeit, this thing was also dying and within two minutes, a full Draco transparent leathery skin lay abandoned on the floor like a discarded army sleeping bag sitting in the corner of the tent waiting to be employed by a tired young soldier. Having shed its skin the creature attempted to stand up and faced Hastings for round two of engagement, and was still heavily fuelled with anger and hatred, yet the beast was getting weaker. Sadly, it was a futile attempt. Erica boldly stepped forward and sprayed at least half the bottle of toxin directly into its face. Then the beast simply stopped breathing and fell silent. It was then that a green glow started to emanate from around the carcass as the corpse slowly shrunk in size and changed into another animal entirely. Erica grabbed the shoulder of Hastings and made an odd statement.

'Kemp, look, it's an grey alien. They must have morphed at some point into this Draco lizard thing. Are we to assume that all these beings are greys.' Hastings kicked the leg of the dead beast to assure himself that it was actually deceased, then answered. 'Erica, I really don't care nor give a piece of lizard shit if this thing is bloody Santa Claus, if these things attack, then they are going to have a very bad hair day indeed. That's all I can say, c'mon let's go destroy this place.'

As Darlene and Erica stepped into the test laboratories in the big blue building, they were overcome by the warm stench of what Darlene would describe as the foul **stench of a rancid fishmonger**, but in this case it would be the odour emanating from an apex predator that roamed the sandy deserts for several days whilst scavaging the landscape for succulent bits of dead meat and carrion it could find. And had obviously never taken time to take a warm soapy bath in order to keep both Darlene or Erica happy. But things were far worse than that, her olfactory senses had gone into deep over drive and she started splurting and sneezing as the fishy aromatic slime crept up the back of her throat and almost dived into her ear canals.

As her beautiful blue eyes started to water and become highly irritated she started gagging and coughing and struggled to clear her throat. Hastings moved forward to stop her and take the lead as they moved closer. 'I'll go first.' He whispered. Darlene was armed with her spray bottle at the ready and as they gazed into the room a single, large clawed talon swiped passed Hastings and caught Darlene across the side of her face casting her to the other side of the corridor.

The mighty tail had done its trick, Hastings on instinct instantly lunged forward at the creature at the same time in response to its attack but was only to be scuppered and thrown to one side as well, and he flew through the air like an old dry bone in a canine free for all munch fest. The beast moved closer and hovered over Darlene as she lay on the floor having suffered a mild bout of concussion.

She instinctively took a large single breath of air whilst staring towards Hastings and shouted out. 'Help me Kemp, this thing is going to kill me.' Hastings stood by almost frozen, almost helpless and watched as the Draco suddenly spat out its long slithering pink tongue to taste the salty skin of the fair maiden. Hastings could see the cold fear in her eyes as the world around her had started to slowly darken as the Dragon's toxic sap and fragrant offensive odour started to numb her skin whilst dulling and shutting down her normal senses.

The Imperial Protector then made another attempt to stand up and fight the beast off to save his friend and colleague. But even with his Shakra membrane fitted his newly found Anunnaki strength was not enough and was still no match for the lizard creature. The serpent had pinned him down like a Queen bee at the annual worker honey making festival with its powerful scaley tail appendage. Erica then leaped onto the back of the beast and struggled with all her might and anger within her, and just managed to stick the syringe straight into the neck of the attacking creature with all her strength then she pushed the plunger of the tube fully in.

But unfortunately, she had missed the jugular vein by an inch and only caught the tough outer leather skinned layer, and the Claw instinctively flicked and twisted its upper body very violently, subsequently casting her aside as if she was a rag doll and a mere inconvenience.

When all seemed to be lost and gloom and doom had made its bed for the long night ahead, there was a shuffling sound in the outside corridor. TA had gone to grab the fire axe from the fire station and had stepped back into the room wielding the big red cleaver above his head. When by an amazing twist of fate and timing the large window at the far end of the office shattered as the wooden framework disintegrated and was ripped apart as a huge hairy four hundred pound, five - foot tall, long haired half hyena and half mongoose carnivore abruptly entered the space. And then it growled out the loudest haunting carnivorous shrieking cries known to man. The unhinged creature was snorting and growling as it spied the Draco lizard dragon standing in the doorway to the room.

Then slowly it started clawing at the wooden flooring, gouging and ripping strips of teak out of the planks of wood as it set itself up for an imminent attack. That was when TA let rip and struck the lizard creature from behind on the left shoulder with the large axe. But, his swipe had simply been deflected.

TA then removed his syringe and held it tightly but was frozen with fright as the two unearthly monsters faced off with one another. The Draco's eyes had become concentrated and as its body tightened up it then stood fully upright, towering to at least seven foot in height. The creature then turned its angry attentions to the arrival of the apex predator and squealed back in response then dropped the dying torso of Darlene to the floor like a sack of potatoes.

After what seemed like a lengthy battle the **An'Goose** laboratory creation by virtue of An'Laara, had pounced at the lizard beast without hesitation and in one violent onslaught of flesh ripping, eye gouging and blood curdling grunts the two creatures were entwined with one another and the deadly deed was soon over.

The An'Goose beast victorious and had killed its prey. The creature then stopped for a moment or two and was panting and sniffing at the cold stale air. The beast then stared back Hastings and TA as if it somehow knew that they were not to be considered a further threat. The hybrid growled then left the building via the gaping hole in the wall where once a nice elegant window had been situated, then began dragging the lifeless, mutilated and savaged remains of the Claw thing along the floor leaving a slimy trail of warm alien blood and a mass of sinews, entrails, shit and no feathers in its wake as it escaped the building.

Hastings and TA assisted by Erica, wasted no time and quickly attended to Darlene and moved her body into the back room of the clinic and laid her down on the medical trolley bed. And in a concerted effort tried desperately to save her from the powerful deadly toxic slime that covered her soft skin. Hastings grabbed a few cloths and found a bottle of white surgical spirit and quite literally soaked a handful of lint in the fluid then started to wipe away the copious coating of vile poison from her mouth, nose, face and chest.

Erica meanwhile had instinctively grabbed the oxygen bottle and firmly placed the orinasal surgical face mask over Darlene's mouth and opened the oxygen valve fully. As the air began to flow out of the mask she watched as Darlene started to slowly respond then they waited patiently. She gave Hastings a very sorrowful glance whilst wiping the tears from her own eyes. Hastings reached over and grabbed her hand tightly. 'I think she will be alright, luckily she is still breathing for now at least.' Erica then reached into her satchel looking for another syringe and pulled out a single yellow flower leaf and played with it in her grip for a few seconds. Hastings then broke the silence.

'What's that for Erica?' He asked pointing at the flower. She responded. 'I found it in the atrium, it was growing under the bench. It was just this one single leaf and flower sitting there, with a short stem, but the odd thing was that it was exactly where I had tested the honeysuckle and sycamore plant mix, it's a mix of nice things for reviving lesser developed or dying plants, and I clearly recall spilling some of the nutrient liquid at the bench and this was the result.

And look I still have that lotus thing that TA gave us back at Hathor,' Hastings stared deeply into her eyes. 'Did you happen to bring any of that nutrient with you?' Erica thrust her hand into her satchel and produced a small blue bottle. 'I did not make much as the sap is very sticky to handle. You don't think that this can be an antidote, do you?' The imperial protector leaned over the bed as Erica handed over the bottle.

'Ninety nine percent of medical breakthroughs in human history are by default, I see no rationale reason not think that is if plants can kill, then they can obviously save as well. I cannot see why nature and your blue bottle mixture is not one of those strange anomalies that serve the plant world.'

He then took a small amount of the sap and carefully spread it across Darlene's lips and waited. Erica went one step further and placed a small dose into one of the syringes and injected it directly into Darlene's arm and bloodstream then smiled. 'Same concoction different method of delivery.'

Outside the medical facility chaos had ensued and the base was in absolute anarchy as the recently arrived back up aliens had left the confides of the basement and had started to attack the human soldiers across the parade square at random. Most of the soldiers tried to either escape conflict or get to the armoury and grab weapons to take control, but the Draco had fused the armoury doors together by heat fusion and entry was futile. The soldiers then resorted to good old face to face hand to chin combat and were almost on an equal footing with the subservient rogue Igigi that served the Draco.

TA had grabbed one of the hand-held remote controls from an alien 'chaperone' entity as he split the creature almost in half with his newly found best friend the humble 'fire axe' and threw the hand device against a nearby brick wall smashing the instrument into a million fragments. He then continued to search for his own Igigi team members. One of which he found lying in the cab of the first truck having obviously succumbed to blunt force trauma as the vehicle smashed through the heavy gates.

In his anger TA had also unwittingly disabled the 'mind control instruments' having tested its durability against the hard stone wall and the real soldiers had been disconnected from the mainframe computer and had started to kick back by attacking the remaining rogue Igigi that were loose in the camp. Hastings had searched the main office but instinctively, knew that Shamgaz and his serpentine lieutenants would not locate themselves near to any major official structure and decided to search the coldest place in the DARPA Barracks. The **morgue** or the **cookhouse**! where the air conditioning would suit their biological needs with a never-ending food supply that could be found as and when required.

He instinctively also knew that the medical facility was a 'no' go area as he had already had an adventure in there. As the protector of the Anunnaki on earth passed by the overturned truck he took great efforts to avoid the tonnage of water that had spilled across the camp and carefully stepped over a couple of rather large fish and a zillion king squid and prawns that were wriggling around the soft sand and were starting to dry out in the diminishing sunlight, he noticed that there were no large dolphins, no sea lions or king penguins not even a single whale were part of the food consignment, and assumed that TA had done something else with them.

If they ever existed at all. Conversely, the vehicle that carried the hybrid beasts was another terrible sight completely. The cab of the Mack truck was almost unrecognisable as it had burst into flames on impact and only the charred outer shell remained.

But the hook -on- trailer itself was also a complete twisted wreck and Hastings presumed that anything that was alive in the tank would have been literally thrown around to a great extent and most definitely suffered serious injury. But now he knew otherwise.

Then he spied three figures moving in the far distance through the black smoke that was still belching around the crash scene and yet he thought that he had caught a glimpse of a **not so much of a beast**. This figure was no Draco lizard creature as he observed earlier when they were attacked. But this was a manly type of figure that was leading his co-conspirators towards one of the aircraft hangars that was highlighted by the large decal lettering on the door depicting - D1.

Just then three military strike aircraft flew over-head at slow speed followed by three heavy duty Chinook helicopters which proceeded to land somewhere in the desert but not too far from the main gates of the installation. Hastings muttered to himself. 'Ahh the cavalry are here at last, typical, always too bloody late.' As he turned to think about his next course of action and hopefully confront who or what he thought this Shamgaz actually was, when he then caught another glimpse of movement to his right-hand side and focussed on the remaining hybrid An'Goose beasts that had emerged from the laboratory building in a hail of loud blood curdling growling and hyena unearthly shrieking.

Each beast firmly holding in their vice grip jaws the lifeless torso of three very dead large lizard humanlike creatures. After, several seconds had passed An'Laara's synthetic pets took flight and fled out of the DARPA complex escaping out into the vast Nevada desert.

The Pentagon had responded swiftly, but oddly, not swiftly enough.

Chapter Thirty – One:

'The Grand Illusion'

Hastings had watched and waited as the huge hangar doors slowly closed together, he spied movement and shadows then heard the distinctive sound of what he thought was a jet engine turbo starting up. The building was being clearly illuminated by the low-level security lights. And then using the cover of the buildings available he managed to negotiate a path to the hangar building without any real physical confrontation or interruption and considering the anarchy that was all around him he did rather well. As the Anunnaki protector approached the side entrance to the huge stainless-steel structure he spied a craft that sat hovering over a large yellow painted circle and was emitting a yellow glow and a dull deep humming sound. The craft appeared to be visually distorting its physical shape and was not unlike the craft he had recently travelled into the land of Lebanon to visit Baalbek.

As he lost his concentration whilst viewing his surroundings for just a few seconds he was suddenly confronted and grabbed by his shoulders by two rather large men each dressed in black three-piece suits, white shirt and wore black tinted glasses that appeared to have small pulsing neon lights at either side of their frames. Then a voice reached his earshot in a distant echo.

'I really do not have much time left here, so I will try and be brief with you. Well done, very well done indeed, I never thought that we could pull this whole thing off, and then again, we did not know how you would react to the wide range of circumstances and events that we put you and the girls through to get here. A very deceptive trail that has led us to this very moment in time. But I can assure you that you are quite safe in here, and let me inform you, that you have served your purpose away beyond any of our expectations.

I am Shamgaz, and the very reason you are here. And I come from the Orion star cluster. Perhaps not the slimy lizard skinned entity you thought I would be. Unlike the soldier server creatures out there. Where, yourself and your accomplices have quite effectively destroyed for us.'

Hastings was somewhat puzzled and very, very, very confused. The human form standing in front of him was not a scaley skinned flesh eating beast that was expected, but that of a fairly tall man creature with normal human features but was dressed to kill in a well fitted charcoal coloured expensive Armani suit. Shamgaz, stood at over six foot in height and was certainly well built and spoke with a calm and very controlled voice almost in an intellectual but lighter tone. 'This meeting had to be carefully engineered with precise calculative outcomes, each element culminating on what we expect to be the best result. Executed in exactly the same way as was Admiral Byrd's encounter with us earlier in the 20th century was. We needed you and your humankind to understand that there is a real **'Alien presence'** on this planet, and other realms which is a place and time that also encompasses this planet and sits within the vast structure of space or indeed the milky way.

But unfortunately, you humans are not equipped to '**see**' the dimensions at work, your frequencies are set much lower to pick up the lesser important rhythms of the afterlife. Hence why you had to engage with the Norske Queen An'Freya and travel within the construct from Hathor, to see for yourself. If not, then you would simply believe that this planet is only visited by physical beings and not multi-dimensional beings such as myself and the other groups of travellers.

Let me explain the why? There is a great war at work between many planets in the heavens, and because of their pride no species will stand down or take a back seat, they cannot admit to any defeat, so they default to out and out aggression. The astral council of five away up there in the stars.' He commented whilst pointing upwards. They talk lot, but they do nothing with their powers to really help things along, and they will simply destroy planets one after the other that refuse to negotiate or agree on the best way forward. Trust me hundreds of colonies are wiped clean out of creation every day. The human construct however is much different. This planet is also '**our**' heaven' And the envy of many colonies, if I may put it that way.

This body is what all planets are trying to replicate, they all want this wonderful environment, but unfortunately for them the Anunnaki were lucky enough to source the third star from the sun and inhabit it first, then ultimately protect it. Then the seven maidens of the planet Pleiadies arrived here on earth under Anunnaki rule to extend the feminine evolution over the seven continents. And for thousands of years they have evolved a species that can and does rival any species in both intellect and ingenuity in the cosmos, well nearly all, the humble human has been a great success story.'

'The Seed': 'Anu – Nexus'

Shamgaz stopped talking for a few seconds and watched as Hastings appeared to try and make sense of his ramblings. 'Are you still with me, not too confused? I know it is a lot to take in, I understand completely? Even for an Anunnaki Imperial Protector and Crusader?' Hastings had relaxed a little more as the two cosmic bouncers stepped back whilst releasing their grip and allowed him to stand freely.

Then Shamgaz continued. 'For the last few hundred years your species have advanced the technology provided and bestowed upon them to such an extent, that the use of these life-saving developments are today being used for mass destruction purposes. And just this last century your species have demonstrated to the outer colonies that earth has developed the capability to reach out beyond the stars and have recently become a real concern. And this destructive path is very evident. The other concern we have is that the earthly human endeavours on Mars are displaying common traits of a colonial overthrow mindset. And that is where the Anunnaki will have to draw the proverbial line in the sand.

Some humans may have to be wiped out! yet again, or the Anunnaki may choose the softer option and only remove the global elite. And they will do it without further question. Mark my words. You see, in the case of Lilith as an example. Let us say that you think you know this entity and that you can trust me here, you do not. You only know 'of her today', and she is rapidly changing, as she has done through the centuries.

This current change is where she has been infected by history and the memory of her monarch an Anunnaki King called Alulu, and she simply wants to take his place on Mars. And nothing we or you can do will ever deter her from achieving this. But the core Anunnaki Pantheon as a collective can.

But her transition will be set in the 4th dimension and not the physical state we find ourselves in today. It is her rogue bastard children that are giving us headaches. She. Lilith is planning a second revolution and intends to overthrow the Martians, and that basically means gaining access to some rather very high spec powerful weapons that not even the Anunnaki themselves wish to even consider using in defence against any planet.

As the consequences of their release are not even worth thinking about. This is also why the keys of Nergal and the energy sources are never brought together on one planet. And that is where our direct intervention has come to a point where the Pleiadian ideology begins and perhaps the demise of earths elite could also begin. It is also a juncture where the Serpent Line and the Anunnaki who have invested their best of interests into this planet for some time. And one day, they intend to live and evolve here amongst humans in complete harmony.

But only when the great Law lords are happy and that all is well. But, then again we have rogue entities like Lilith to deal with. The so-called release of weapons on Mars **was not a real event** and the messages were conveyed by my colleague TA, to your good self and An'Mer directly.

Which as far as you are concerned was complete misdirection and a part of the **grand illusion**. We had to get Lilith to acknowledge that Mars was actually under physical attack and the Draco who are not present on earth had also brought nuclear weapons to the planet. And look around you, here we are, but with no weapons. But, in real terms we did blow up a few clusters of asteroids that were hanging around the great bear constellation as a sign of some sort of disruption. And Lilith had reacted as anticipated. But the unannounced arrival of the underworld Norske Queen An'Freya, was certainly a turn up for the books, as we thought it was too much of an ask, but she did. We never suspected that the great Triad would ever be evoked, but she does serve another purpose. She An'Freya will ultimately control Lilith and keep her boxed up in the fourth or fifth dimension, and even Hathor can watch over Lilith within her own domain.

Well at least until such times as the Anunnaki take full command of the heavens again. Incidentally, I do have the Axum keys of Nergal, your covenant stones here with me. We knew that Lilith would understand the consequences of their removal from the earthly temple. TA will arrange for you to return them to their human keepers. As I also understand that you are protected from their radiation sources and can handle them safely. I am sure the Pleiadians will also assist you.

The other part of this great conundrum, however, is the most important one, and that was we had to not only find the Merlithian colony but to somehow get the Merlithian off the planet. As they would have destroyed the Igigi, the humans and probably my presence if they had advanced here to DARPA. Even more so, they will have destroyed this human laboratory in this political house of Frankenstein. We also knew the Merlithian as a colony existed somewhere. But, in essence we had no real idea where, and if An'Mer and An'Laara are anything like their maternal mother Lilith then they are both a serious deadly threat to the cosmos as was King Alulu in Anunnaki memory.

And now we know that An'Mer was going to be potentially a very serious problem.' Hastings opened up his hands and blinked his eyes a few times then asked another question. 'So, this complete charade, this mass scale deception plan was simply to find the location of the Merlithian colony, is that really it?

'The Seed': 'Anu – Nexus'

Was it really that simple, I mean you could have just flown to Ararat and destroyed them there and then in one swift assault!'

Shamgaz, raised both his hands in the air, then gave him a very long enduring stare of contemplation and then responded. 'Creation is a balance of keeping things in order, there are a great many rules to follow and they must never be broken. An example being that An'Mer is the final prime '**seed**' of a powerful Anunnaki king entity and there will be a plan for his Anunnaki succession journey.

Remember we are dabbling with the **great Anu** and his Anunnaki bloodline lineage. To destroy without cause is never going to be a good thing. The great powers and the warlords dwelling in the house of heavens are watching our every move and record every breath we take. 'You do not realise it yet, but, you yourself and the girls have been very instrumental in stabilising not only a physical world by removing these Nephilim beasts from existence but, have also provided very much needed breathing space in order to keep balance in the heavens together.

If An'Mer was ever permitted to execute Lilith's plan, then he would have taken control of the keys of Nergal and eventually overthrew Lilith and rightfully take over the planet Mars himself and forge his own new empire. That outcome is not on the Anunnaki agenda as Mars is being constructed to provide a safe habitat for humans in the distant future.

So, something had to be done. And who better to execute the plan than mankind themselves, albeit, with a nudge of hybrid astral intervention of course. This is not some child's nursery or parlour game we are playing. This is how the heavens operate. Remember it is not just yourself that has prevailed here, but your colleagues as well. The Pleiadian especially 'Darlene' she has been acting unwittingly as our direct communications conduit to ensure we are successful.

And that was her purpose in life, first endure a physical lifetime of existence and then just for a few split seconds of significant impact time do what is required. And then of course, the graceful Arcturian Erica, well, she was the very intellectual tool that **helped** destroy the very creature that the human scientists created.

You must understand Hastings that we are the serpentine colony and are all natural grey aliens, or in your understanding core Pleiadians. And we do not always reside on our home planets as a mono-species. We are the collective vibrational elements of creation. You observe me at this moment in your time as a physical state of being, but in reality, I am a compendium of matter, energy, light and vibration, and we can shapeshift into the physical realm at any time. But that despicable concoction of chemicals that the military humans placed within the DNA strands of those recovered bodies in Iraq. Well, that was absolute defiance of the natural evolution process.

Imagine, if they somehow had started to breed, I mean that would be catastrophic. Firstly, because they were not pure Draco and certainly not Anunnaki. And, we could have never reversed engineered their make up at this stage even if we wanted to. So, a quick termination strategy was engineered, it was that simple. But, before we do depart company An'Hastings remember the Anunnaki cannot always move between the physical and the vibrational worlds, but, you can, especially since the shakra harnesses were introduced by the Merlithian to you all. That was when we had our break moment and tuned into every move and body frequency changes that the Merlithian made around you. And of course, you are now part of the shakra construct. I am sure we will talk again in the near future.

But you must acknowledge that you or your colleagues will never understand the real reason why? of course. An'Mer and the Merlithian colony are not really disruptive beings per se and are certainly not hostile, but, it was because of their maternal mother Lilith being a social tyrant that they were simply duped or tricked into a world of fantasy that they could not imagine was false. And subsequently, they did her very bidding. As Lilith actually believed after millenia of secretive planning that her designs of planet domination was in jeopardy.

An'Mer has been used and abused by design for cosmic reasons. And he will only have Lilith to blame for his capture. He and the colony will return to Nibiru, but they will be re-engineered to ensure that the **Enki plan** for your humankind succession is maintained for all time. And furthermore, for some strange reason the earthbound An'Laara the bioscientist, well we think she has gone missing, but I am sure there will be a logical explanation somewhere for that. You have served us well.'

Chapter Thirty - Two:

'Setting the records Straight'

After the departure of Shamgaz from DARPA, Hastings had met up with his colleagues and were all subsequently placed under arrest and met by the higher echelons of the military intelligence services. The team were transported off the DARPA complex under a military escort and flown to a location where top officials wanted to meet with them in a neutral environment. The group were then separated and interviewed one by one.

Hastings had initially met with General George Dundee from the Military Sciences Arm of the Pentagon for an informal styled interview under the close scrutiny of the internal cameras and an armed guard. The officer stood at six foot two and was dressed in civilian attire comprising of a dark blue Armani suit, black brogue shoes, white shirt and had donned gold rimmed reading glasses. Just before he laid down the document that he was reading onto the desk the officer then dismissed the guard.

'A very good morning Mister Hastings, I trust we are treating you in a manner that suits your taste. 'Hastings then spontaneously responded. 'If you mean apart from being locked up and isolated as a common criminal or prisoner, then I will say no, I am not being treated very well, and how are my colleagues?' The General loosened his necktie and leaned across the desk then spoke very softly ensuring that his lip movements were not recorded on the CCTV.

'We can do this the easy way or the hard way, it is entirely up to you. Mister Hastings, we cannot let you go back into society without a formal face to face discussion, the girls are fine presently, and this is not a good cop or bad cop shit chit chat either. We do not know why you were at DARPA, and that gives us some real concerns. And we know that your involvement in recent events are of both a technical and political nature and dare I say alien to the concepts of what they do at DARPA, and political spying or espionage is such a serious crime to day in this political climate.

So, please tell me why you and those two ladies were caught inside a top security scientific installation run by the American government?' Hastings smiled a very broad grin. 'Well George, may I call you George?' The General smiled. 'Of course.' He replied. 'You see General George we were at DARPA because the big nasty political men in this world that you call Presidents and Kings and other imperial pompus names have upset a few alien species in the outer galaxy, and we were 'beamed' down into the base just like on star trek. We are here in order to remove some **alien home grown toxic entities** that your ever so silly government people had physically created a monster using some very rogue and dubious DNA tests, under a project, let us call it **'skin-tight'** just for fun of keeping things simple shall we.

And dear oh, dear George! You let them escape and upset the very 'Little green men' that are controlling your nation in the form of a species called the Igigi people, and Not Anunnaki. Are you with me so far George, because I have a story that will boil your brainbox.'

The General then sat back in his chair and shaking his head. 'You know I have just read the most interesting account of DARPA from my General Staff officer assigned to operations at the laboratories and also a top-secret memo from SETI our listening station. 'Hastings clasped his hands together then made a request. 'George, can I stop you there, can I get a rather large mug of coffee, milk and sugar please, you HAD better get one as well, because I certainly think you are going to need it.' After the drinks arrived the General was still staring at Hastings very strangely then posed a question.

'You know Mister Hastings we at the Pentagon deal with some very strange stuff and we are wondering why your name appeared on an electronic communications signal that came from what SETI believe to be a signal from a planet in the Orion cluster, I mean really, what is that all about?'

Hastings took a sip of his coffee and then smirked. 'Well, George, an easy question to answer, that is because I did, I made a call from Baalbek in the Lebanon using an alien Ankh and a large lump of granite, I mean mobile phone technology these days.' The look on the general's face said it all. 'And before you ask the who or the what George the signal was indeed bounced around the ionosphere a wee bit.

Well c'mon on your a military man, you know what satellites and older style telephones can be like.' As the two fell into a humorous style of conversation their talk was interrupted and brought to a sharp halt as the Chief of Staff Officer of 'Cyclan' according to his name tag grabbed the General's attention and handed over a mobile phone to the Commander.

After a very brief and quiet conversation the General, took a rather large breath, then passed the phone back to the Chief of Staff. He then gave Hastings a quick glance, picked up his coffee and left the interview room without saying another word. Thirty minutes or so later and the trio Erica Vine, Darlene Gammay and Kemp Hastings were being transported by what Kemp would describe as a Pleiadian utility craft and were apparently heading to the lands of **Ethiopia** with a valuable cargo to set the world religious records straight.

End

Post-Script
Quotes from across the web: Google.

There is an agreement between the United States Government and the alien cooperation and agreements which had been signed by the species including an underground base in the depths of Mars, where aliens and human select astronauts work together.

- *They have been waiting for humanity to develop and reach a stage where we will understand in general what space and spaceships are? Eshed said: Referring to the intergalactic Federation*

- *Alien experts believe they have found an ancient pyramid on Mars, citing NASA rover photos as their evidence. UFO hunter and conspiracy theorists believes the Red Planet once hosted advanced alien civilisations. In his latest bizarre discovery, theorists claim to have found evidence of a pyramid and two alien faces buried in the rusty sands of Mars. The discovery sparked some excitement from UFO enthusiasts who believe it could be the real deal.*

- *The Great Pyramid of Giza may create large quantities of electromagnetic energy in certain chambers of its structure, according to a research published in the Journal of Applied Physics by Russian and German academics.*

- *The position of Khufu's Great Pyramid has been questioned countless times. This pyramid, according to one theory, was erected exactly in the middle of an energy hotspot on telluric ley lines.*

- *Analyze - the crisis and rationale behind the Anunnaki decision to nuke 5 cities in the Jordan plain, resulting in the obliteration of Sumerian civilization. Draws upon the work of Zecharia Sitchin, the Book of Genesis, Sumerian clay tablets, and archaeological evidence such as ancient radioactive skeletons.*

- *Examines the Anunnakis' lack of higher consciousness, their reliance on technology, their sacred power objects and sacred geometry, and the possibility of Anunnaki bases on Mars in the distant past*

- *Two of Enlil's attacks against the Enki clan and humanity are described in the stories of the Deluge and the Tower of Babel. His final attempt, after coercing the Assembly of the Gods into voting yes, was the nuclear bombing of 5 cities of the Jordan plain, including Sodom and Gomorrah, which resulted in the destruction of the Sumerian civilization and the Anunnakis' own civilization on Earth, including their space port in the Sinai. The author reveals how, after each attempt, humanity was saved by Enki, chief scientist Ninmah, and Enki's son Hermes.*

End.

Printed by Libri Plureos GmbH in Hamburg, Germany